HEATHER and BROOM

Tales of the Scottish Highlands

HEATHER
and BROOM

Tales of the Scottish Highlands

SORCHE NIC LEODHAS

Illustrated by Consuelo Joerns

HOLT, RINEHART AND WINSTON
New York/Chicago/San Francisco

LIBRARY OF CONGRESS CATALOG CARD NUMBER: 60-13073
Published, September, 1960
Seventh Printing, October, 1969

SBN:03–035280–0

This book is for

JENIFER JILL DIGBY

Introduction

WHEN SOMEONE TELLS YOU a Scottish story and you ask where it came from, he may say, "I had it from my father, and he had it from his father." But sometimes the answer will be, "My father had it from a storyteller that came by one time." Or "There was an old bochad (fellow) that used to come by, telling stories, and my grandmother had the tale from him." These last will be seanachie stories.

The first seanachies were the monks. As they were the only ones who knew how to write, they kept the records, and wrote down the ancient history of Scotland. They were not storytellers, but story collectors. There was as much fiction as fact in what they wrote, so the old manuscripts were mostly collections of stories.

The harpers learned some of the stories. They went about from one castle or manor to another with the old stories and with new ones that they made up themselves, about stirring events which they heard about as they traveled. They did not tell their stories, but sang them to the music of the Gaelic harp which could be carried on the arm. They were called bards sometimes, but they were seanachies of a sort.

I do not know when the seanachies of the later times began to come along, but it probably was around 1600, for before that it was not easy for a common man to leave his village and go wandering about. There were laws which made him stay in his own parish or on the estate to which he belonged. But about that time seanachies began to appear at fairs and at festive gatherings of the people. Some of them only told their stories, but there were a few who sold them, in small leaflets or on sheets of paper. Then they began to go about, not to the great houses, but to the small villages and lonely shielings (cottages) telling their stories for a meal and a night's lodging.

There were a few stories about clan chieftains which had an historical source, but these wandering seanachies suited their stories to the people to whom they were told, so they are cottage or household stories for the most part. And even the historical stories have in them, almost always, some sort of fairy person.

There were still seanachies going about during the 1800's. There were seanachies in Perthshire in 1830, and in Athole, and some of the counties of the northern and western Highlands in the 1850's. I have heard there was one in Nova Scotia, going about telling tales as late as 1890.

Some of the stories traveled far, for the people who heard them remembered them and told them again, carrying the stories along with them wherever they went. All the seanachie stories that I know were told to me here in America. I have never met a seanachie, and think probably the automobile, the cinema, and the radio put them out of business.

The eight stories in this collection are all seanachie stories.
The Ailpein Bird, the Stolen Princess, and the Brave Knight:

8

probably the oldest, and a legend of the MacAlpine clan.
Brought from Argyllshire.
The Woman who Flummoxed the Fairies: A household story,
brought from Durris near Aberdeen.
The Lairdie with the Heart of Gold: A clan story, supposed to
be told of one of the Grants. Brought from above Inverness
and just north of Culloden Field.
The Gay Goss-Hawk: A version of the ballad, from Perthshire.
The Lass that Couldn't Be Frighted: Also a household story,
brought from Durris.
The Daughter of the King Ron: A legend of Clan Donald
(MacDonald of the Isles).

There are other seal legends about the MacDonalds. One
which is often told traces the origin of the clan; tells about a
MacDonald, who, fleeing from his enemies into exile in the
Western Isles, took a seal woman he found there for his wife,
and their descendants became the later MacDonalds.
Spin, Weave, Wear: A household story from Durris.
The Bogles from the Howff: The most modern of the stories,
brought from Blairgowrie, north and west of Dundee.

The main difference between Highland and Lowland Scottish tales is in the style of the telling. Highland tales have a rhythm that can almost be scanned, like verse. Ends of sentences frequently have a cadence that falls, caused by an unaccented syllable at the end of the last word, which could cause a singsong effect but miraculously doesn't. It is more noticeable in the serious stories than in the merry ones, but even the household tales have a Gaelic lilt to them. And I think the Highland tales have a more poetic quality than those from below the border.

Lowland tales are told in a matter-of-fact, plain-spoken fashion, with little ornament to them, and they march along, while Gaelic stories seem to dance.

I like both Highland and Lowland stories, in spite of these differences.

Highlanders and Lowlanders seem to have a different attitude toward fairy people. The persons in the Lowland stories appear to flee them, fear them, and fight against them. They are supernatural persons, held in superstitious dread.

To the Highlander the fairy folk are simply a different race of people. In the Highland stories the human beings live with them and among them in intimacy and usually amicably. They regard them with amusement or affection, and if occasionally it comes to a battle there is no grudge carried afterward. There is a feeling of forbearance on both sides.

Contents

HEATHER and BROOM

Tales of the Scottish Highlands

The Ailpein Bird, the Stolen Princess, and the Brave Knight

ONCE IN THE OLD TIMES, the Good Times, when there were kings in Scotland, there was a wee Scottish princess who was stolen away from her father's castle. It was during a raid by a wicked king from another land she was taken, and her father never knew she was gone till the battle was over. Then someone came running to him, to tell the king she was lost, and the alarm was given. They searched the castle from end to end and all around it, too, but none of them found a trace of her.

By the time she was missed, the wicked king and his men were far away, and the princess over the saddle of one of their steeds wrapped in a soldier's cloak.

It was not to capture the princess that the raid was made, but to take her father's castle, for the wicked king wanted to kill her father and reign in his stead. Her father was a good king and ruled his people well, so his land prospered and he had plenty of gold.

The castle stood fast, and the wicked king and his men were driven away and had to go back to their own land without any of the gold. But as they went, one of the king's men caught up the princess and took her along instead.

When they got back home the little princess was brought before the wicked king, and he looked her over. He saw that she was beautiful, and as he was angry because he'd lost the battle he made up his mind to keep her, to pay her father back for the beating he'd got.

He had her put among the women of his castle, and nobody but himself and his men-at-arms knew who she was; and they would not dare to tell, for he said he'd have their lives if they did.

So the poor little princess stayed in the wicked king's castle. She was not ill-treated, for they all liked her well enough, but she was unhappy, for her heart was sick for the sight of her own land and her own people. Her father could not come and get her, for he did not know where she was. He had them search for her for many a day, but at last he gave up hope of ever finding out what had happened to her and mourned her as dead.

When a year had gone by the wicked king sent for the princess. He had a black thought in his mind: to marry her to his son. He knew that he couldn't get the gold he wanted by capturing her father's castle, for he'd already tried that and it didn't come out the way he wanted. So the next best thing would be to marry his son to the little princess, and use her to pry some of the gold out of her father.

The princess came and stood before the king, and he told her what he had in his mind. She said nothing to him against it, for she knew she'd better not. But her heart sank at the thought of marrying the king's son. He was proud and cold, and she was pretty sure he was cruel, too. She thought there was nothing she wouldn't give to be at home, and safe in her father's house again.

That day the women robed her in costly velvet and put

16

jewels on her neck and wrists and fingers, and she was sent down to have dinner at the king's table, for all the world to see. She sat at the king's right hand at dinner, with the king's son at her other side, and when they rose from the table, she was told to stay in the hall with the ladies of the king's court.

While they were gathered there together a wandering harper came into the hall to sing to them. He looked the company over as he sang, and he saw the little princess sitting there. He looked at her once, and he thought she was beautiful. He looked at her twice, and thought she was much too sad for one so young. But with the third look, he said to himself, "I've seen that face before!" Where or when he couldn't tell, but he knew it was in some other, happier place.

He had been singing songs men like to hear, of warlike deeds and brave heroes, so now he sang a song for the ladies. It was a light, merry song, and the princess remembered that she had heard it before in her own land, and she smiled, remembering. It was only a wee ghost of a smile, but the harper saw it, and then he knew who she was!

There had been another king's castle he had sung in long ago, and she was the daughter of the king there and the merriest one of the court. When she smiled, everyone smiled with her. When she laughed, it was a treat to hear her! She was a bit of a lassie then, not grown up as she was now, for it was a long time ago. He had come back to that castle about a month back, and the servants there told him that the king would have no music in the castle, for he was mourning the princess who had disappeared during a battle about a year ago. Everybody said she was dead, poor lass, and their king's heart was broken by the loss of her.

The harper told himself that he'd lay his life on the odds that this was the same princess, and she wasn't dead at all!

And he wondered what she was doing here, in this unlikely place. But he was too wise to say aloud what he thought. He was sure there was something wrong about it.

When they'd had enough of his singing the harper was sent to the servant's hall, and there he was given food and shown a place where he could sleep for the night. The king sent a man to tell him he was pleased with the singing, and that the harper was to stay at the castle and sing to them again.

While he was eating, the harper questioned the servants about the princess, but who she was or where she came from nobody could tell him. She had been at the castle for as long as a year, and now she was going to marry the king's son in about a month's time.

The harper wrapped himself in his cloak and lay down where they told him to. But he did not sleep, nor did he stay at the castle. Long before the wind of dawn had whistled in a new day he had taken his harp upon his arm and silently slipped away. He passed by the drowsy guards, and they saw that it was only the harper and let him go on.

The harper took the shortest road to the princess' father's castle, and he ate where he could and slept when he had to, and at last, toward the eve of the fourth day he came to its gates. The guards there were surprised to see him back, for he had not been allowed to sing the last time, but when he insisted and would not let them turn him away one of them agreed to take him into the hall. As for the rest, whether he might sing or not, that was up to the king.

The king frowned when he saw the harper, for music reminded him of his daughter who had a way of singing all day long. Then he relented for he thought of the people of the court and how little pleasure there was for them nowadays. So he called the harper to him and told him that he might sing, but must wait until the king himself had gone away. Then the king started toward the door of the hall, but the harper placed himself in his path and kneeling before him said, "Your Majesty would not leave if he knew the song I sing is one written for him alone. Let your Majesty remain in the hall and hear if it be not strange and wonderful, and judge of its importance to himself."

The king was a man of great courtesy and he was touched that the harper had sought to please him by making a song for him, for he had been told that the guards had turned him away the last time he came. He would listen to the song he told the harper.

The harper struck a chord on his harp and then he began to sing. He sang of a castle (like this one) besieged by an enemy in the dark of a winter's night. He sang of the flashing of swords, and the clashing of spears, and of bowmen on the walls. He sang of the enemy driven away, and of the quiet after the battle.

Then soft his voice grew and gentle, as the harper sang of a fair young princess who was her father's dear joy. After the battle was over the princess was not in her bower, nor could she be found in the castle, but never was seen again.

When the harper came to this part of the song the king sat up in his chair. He looked like a man who would have wept, had not all his tears run dry. He would have stopped the harper and he frowned and lifted his hand, but the harper said, "The end is not yet!" and hurried on with his song. And now he sang of another castle, in the kingdom of the enemy king who had led his men in the battle on that dark winter's night. He sang of a fair young princess in that wicked king's castle, blooming like a wild rose in a wilderness. Captive was she and there was sorrow in her eyes, for she was fated to

19

marry the son of the enemy king, who was as wicked as the king himself.

"Who is the white rose blooming in the wilderness, captive and despairing, far from her own home?" sang the harper.

And the princess' father gave a great cry, and jumped from his chair. He seized the harper by the arm and dashed his harp to the ground. His eyes flashed and his face was terrible, and he shouted, "Who? Who? harper, *tell me her name!*"

The harper was not daunted by the king. He looked the king straight in the eyes, and the name he spoke was that of the king's lost daughter.

Then rose a shout of rejoicing from all the court assembled that made the whole castle ring. And all the people who were not in the hall came running, and when they heard the news they, too, rejoiced. From highest to the lowest, there had not been such happiness upon the faces of the king's people since the princess had been stolen away.

The king vowed that he would raise such an army as never had been seen before, and march against the castle of the wicked king and fetch his daughter home!

Now at the court there was a brave young knight who had loved the princess long. And when he heard what his king said there was a great fear in his heart that when the wicked king saw the army approach, he would know it was the father of the princess coming to fetch her home, and therefore might do the little princess some harm. He told the other knights his thought, and, as many of them agreed, with him they went to the king, and after much argument persuaded him to let the young knight go first in disguise and try to bring the princess away. When she was safely away he would let the king know, and the army could march against the wicked king's castle.

There were at that time many friars going about from place

to place, begging their way as they went, and they were well received in all places, being holy men. So the brave young man dressed himself in a coarse brown habit with a great cowl over his head, and taking a wallet over his shoulder and a staff in his hand he started out as one of these friars to rescue the princess.

The very day that the knight started on his journey the princess sat at dinner between the wicked king and his son. While they were eating, an Ailpein bird flew in through one of the tall windows seeking refuge from the force of the winter wind.

The people in the hall jumped up in terror, and shouted, "An ill omen! An ill omen!" for it was thought to be a sign of ill luck when a bird flew into a castle in that way. The king told the guard to shoot the bird, but it flew straight to the princess. She caught the bird in her arms and clasped it to her breast, and then she turned and faced the soldier bravely. He had lifted his crossbow to shoot the bird, but he lowered it, for he could not kill the bird without killing the princess, too.

"Let her keep it, then," said the king, "since she fancies it." For he was good-natured from the wine he had drunk, and from the thought of the gold he was going to get through the princess after he had married her to his son. " 'Tis only a white falcon strayed from its keeper in the stress of the storm," he added. "Let her have it! 'Twill do for her to fondle until she has something better to fill her arms." He looked at his son, and winked and laughed, and sipped at his wine again.

The Ailpein bird nestled in the princess' arms, and when she returned to her room to sleep she took it with her. When her serving-woman had gone, she pulled the cover from her window and set the bird upon the sill. She sat upon the wide sill

21

beside it and stroked its head gently and said, "There, pretty bird, go on your way, for the storm is over and I would not have you a prisoner as I am."

And she wept and said, "Ah me, that I had wings to fly to my father's house!"

Then the Ailpein bird spoke to her and said, "I cannot take you to your father's house, for I must return to my own land. But I can take you from this castle, for you may come with me if you will."

"I will gladly go wherever you take me!" said the princess.

She dropped her velvet gown upon the floor and laid the jewels they had given her upon it. She put on the dress she had worn when they carried her off, and then she was ready to go.

The Ailpein bird opened out his wings, and as he stretched them to their full span he grew before her eyes until he filled the whole space of the wide window. The princess stepped to the window ledge and seated herself upon his back, and away the white bird flew. He flew over field and forest and mountain, and soon the dark, sleeping castle was far behind them.

By dawn they had passed the borders of the wicked king's kingdom and three other kingdoms beside, and by nightfall they had left all the kingdoms of the world behind them and had come to a strange white land where all was a wilderness of ice and snow and in the midst of it an immense white castle.

"Here we will spend the night," said the Ailpein bird.

A great snowy owl was the lord of this castle, and when the two birds met, they greeted each other fondly. The princess was given food to eat, and put to sleep in a bed of feathers, so warm that she never thought once of the coldness of that land.

The next morning she seated herself again upon the back

of the Ailpein bird, and they took up their journey once more. All day they flew and at the end of the day they came to a strange land of fire. The skies were red with the flames of it and the earth rolled and heaved like the waves of a boiling sea. The bird took a sure way above the clouds of smoke and steam till he came to a huge black castle that stood upon the top of a tall black mountain.

"We will stay here for the night," said the Ailpein bird.

A great black raven was the lord of this castle, and the two birds met like brothers long parted. The princess was fed and put to bed in a room where the wings of many birds fanned her all through the night, so that she never gave a thought to the heat from the plains below.

On the morning of the third day the princess and the Ailpein bird set out again, and toward evening they came to a tall mountain with steep shining sides of glass. It was so high that the top of it was hidden in the clouds of the heavens. But when they had passed over it, they came to a fair green land that stretched as far as the eye could see. The land was full of bird song, for many a tree grew on that plain and every tree was full of singing birds. In the midst of the plain rose a great golden castle that shone like the sun, but without the heat of it. Here the Ailpein bird set the princess down.

"This is my castle," said the Ailpein bird, "for I am the king of all the birds. Here you will be safe, and we will try to make you happy."

So the princess lived in the golden castle, and was happy with the birds, except for the great longing that was still in her heart to be at home with her father and her own people.

Now, when the princess had reached the castle of the snowy owl the brave young knight who set out to rescue her had gone a third of his way. When she came to the castle of the black

23

raven he had only a third of his journey left to go. But when she reached the golden castle, the young knight reached the castle of the wicked king at the very same moment.

The gate of the castle stood before him, so he pulled the cowl of his friar's robe over his head till it shadowed his face. There was no guard at the gate, so the knight went in and found the servant's hall as the friars were used to do. Everything seemed to be in a grand turmoil in the castle, with people hurrying in and out. The servants were huddled together at one end of the servants' hall. The young knight went up to them and asked what all the bother was about. He looked like a friar, so they thought he was one, and told him their troubles at once. There had been a fair young princess staying in the castle and she had disappeared. It was three days ago they had missed her, and the king was in a terrible rage, for she was to have married his son, and the king's heart had been set on the marriage. When he was angry he was terrible, and nobody knew what he'd do. Where had she gone? Well, how could anyone say? The king had the guards thrown into the dungeon, for he said she must have slipped by them while they were sleeping. But all the guards were honest men, and they all swore that not one of them had closed an eye all night. Only the king wouldn't believe them. She was gone and that was sure, for there wasn't a hole or corner the king hadn't had them dig into, from the cellars to the garrets of the castle, and if she'd been anywhere they'd have found her.

The knight went and sat down on a bench by the fireplace, to ponder about it. What he was to do now he just did not know. If he went out after her which way should he go? If he stayed here and they couldn't find her he'd waste time he could have spent hunting for her. If they found her and brought her back he'd never be able to take her away, for the king would watch her closer than ever then.

An old woman came into the kitchen and she came over and sat down at the other end of the bench. The knight looked up at her once, but he paid no more attention to her. He was too busy thinking. But after a while he noticed the old woman was edging closer and closer to him, and pretty soon she was right up beside him. He looked at her again and she said, "Father, I haven't confessed my sins for a long time. Will you hear me?"

The knight didn't want to do that, for of course he wasn't really a friar and had no right to. But while he was wondering how to get out of it, the old woman began to whisper to him, as if she were telling him her sins. But she wasn't! What she did say nearly made him jump out of his skin.

"I know who you are!" said she, and she laid a hand on his arm, as if to warn him to be careful. "You are no friar, but a knight come to rescue the princess. I am the woman who attended her and I can help you." Then the old woman told him that it was the Ailpein bird who had carried the princess away, and if he meant no evil toward the princess, she would tell him how he could go after her.

"There is no evil in my heart," said the knight proudly, "only a desire to serve my lady and my king."

" 'Tis a long journey," the old woman told him. "There will be great danger along the way."

"Tell me how I must go," said the knight, disregarding her words, "and I will start at once."

The old woman felt in her pocket and took something out. It was three white feathers, and she put them in his hand. "Take these," said she. "I found them on the floor of the room

25

when I went to dress her in the morning, and saw she was gone. Something told me they were nothing common so I hid them away, and when I had time I took them to a wise woman I know in the village outside of the castle. It was she who told me where the princess had gone and who had taken her. She told me to keep the feathers safe for you would come, and then, if you were not afraid to go after her, I was to give them to you."

"I am not afraid!" said the knight.

"You will have to go to the end of the kingdoms of the world," said the old woman, "for that is what the wise woman said. And when you get there keep on going straight ahead, no matter what lies in your path. As for the feathers you must put them safely away, for they will help you in your hour of need."

The knight put the feathers in his wallet. Then he asked the old woman where he could find a trusty runner, to take a message to the princess' father.

"I am going away from here," said the old woman, "for I will stay no longer in this wicked place. I waited only to tell you what the wise woman said. But I have the keys to the dungeon, and before I go, I shall let the guards out because they told the truth. One of them will take your message for you."

So they arranged to meet outside the castle, and when the woman came, she had one of the guards with her. The knight gave him a message, to tell the princess' father that the princess was gone from there and he could bring on his army if he liked. As for the knight, he was going to find the princess and fetch her home.

So the guard ran off with the message and the old woman went with the knight to the end of the forest and showed him

the road he'd have to take. "Where will you go?" asked the
knight as they parted.

"If your king is a good king, as you say he is," said the old
woman, "I shall go there, and wait till you bring the princess,
and then I can serve her again." And with that she turned her
back and went into the forest again, while the knight started
out on his way to find the princess.

He traveled out of that kingdom and into the next, and on
and on through one after another. He had no trouble finding
food or a place to lay his head at night, for everyone he came
to thought he was a friar, so they gave what he wanted without his having to ask for it. But at last he came to the edge of
the kingdoms of the world, and there before lay the great land
of ice.

He stepped out onto the ice and started across it, for he had
to go straight ahead as the wise woman had said. But the ice
shifted under his feet and great blocks of it hurled themselves
across his path, while frost clouds bit at him like forest wolves
and the cold struck through to his bones. He thought he
would perish there and never see the princess again. Then
he thought of the feathers the old woman had given him! He
took the first one out, and as soon as he held it in his hand it
turned into a soft white cloak. He wrapped the cloak about
him and he felt the cold no longer. The fields of ice grew still
and the frost clouds drew away from him, and he came safe
to the great white castle.

The snowy owl met him at the door, and the knight begged
leave of him to come in and break his fast and rest before he
traveled on.

"You may come in," said the snowy owl, "but before you eat
or sleep you must strive with me to see which is the strongest."

With that he struck his beak thrice on the floor and his

28

feathers fell away. He stepped out of them, a tall young man with red-gold hair, in the pride of his strength.

So the two of them grappled and the struggle began. All through the night they fought and the walls of the castle rocked and groaned with the greatness of their striving. But when day broke, neither of them had bested the other.

"Hold!" said the red-haired man. " 'Tis enough! For we are equals and neither of us has won. By that I know there is no evil in you. Now I shall take you for a brother and I will help you."

The snowy owl took on his feathers again and had food and drink brought. While the knight was eating he told the owl his story.

"The Ailpein bird was here not long ago," said the snowy owl. "And there was a fair lady with him. If she is the one you seek I will help you on your journey when you have rested."

All that day the knight slept well and warm in the cloak of feathers. At nightfall the owl woke him and told him to leave the cloak behind for he would no longer need it. He took the knight on his back and carried him to the end of the land of the ice, and there he set him down.

"I can go no farther," said the snowy owl. "Farewell brother! You must go on alone." And back he flew to his own white castle.

The knight looked ahead, and there before him stretched the land of fire, heaving and boiling and spurting flames and sending clouds of smoke and steam to the sky. There was no road at all to travel across it.

The knight took the second feather out of his wallet, and as soon as he held it in his hand it began to grow and turned into a great white plume that lifted him up above the fire and the smoke and the steam.

29

At nightfall it set him down at the door of the huge black castle on the top of the tall black mountain. At the door stood the great black raven, and when the knight begged leave to come in and break his fast and rest, the raven told him he might come in, but that he should not eat nor rest until they had striven to find out which was the stronger.

Then the raven struck his beak thrice on the floor and his feathers dropped away, and out from them stepped a tall man with black hair in the pride of his strength. The two of them grappled, and all night long they fought, while the walls of the castle shook and strained with the might of their struggle and the smoke whirled through the hall so fiercely that they could scarcely see each the other's faces.

When day broke neither of them had bested the other. Then the raven cried, "Hold! 'Tis enough! You have not won, nor have I. Now we are equals, and I shall take you for a brother and I will help you." Then he took his feathers on again, and had food and drink brought. While the knight ate, he told the raven his story.

The raven said that the Ailpein bird had been there not long before with a fair young lady. "If she is the one you seek," said the raven, "I will help you on your way when you have rested."

The knight slept all day in the raven's castle, while the wings of many birds kept the heat of the fires below away. At nightfall the raven woke him and took him on his back to the end of the land of fire. But the great plume he left behind, for the raven told him he would need it no longer.

The raven set him down and said, "Farewell brother! I can go no farther with you. You must go on alone." Then the raven stretched his wings and returned to his own black castle.

The knight looked before him, and there before him was a

great plain, and from the plain rose a mountain so high that its top was hidden in the clouds of the sky. He stepped out and traveled across the plain, and at nightfall he came to the mountain. Then he saw that the steep sides of the mountain were made of shining glass, and no man could hope to climb it.

The knight took the last feather out of his wallet, and it turned under his hand into a white wain with spiked wheels. He got into the wain and it started to climb up the mountain. All night the wain climbed, by the light of the stars and the moon. Up the mountain it went and through the clouds and down the other side. When day broke it came to the bottom and stopped. The knight stepped out of it and looked ahead of him. There before him was the wide green plain with its trees full of singing birds, and up from the trees rose the shining golden castle. And the knight knew that he had come to the end of his journey.

The Ailpein bird stood at the door of the castle when the knight came up to it. He greeted the knight courteously and asked him why he had come to the kingdom of the birds.

"I have come to take the princess back to her father," the knight told him.

"That she must decide for herself," said the Ailpein bird.

He sent for the little princess and she came at once. When she saw the knight her tears flowed from her eyes for joy, at seeing one who came from her own home. But she smiled through her tears for joy, too.

"This knight has come to take you home," said the Ailpein bird. "And though I love you well and would have you stay, I have not forgotten that you saved my life at the risk of your own, so I will not keep you if you would go."

The princess looked long into the Ailpein bird's eyes. "I

31

love you well," said she, "even as you love me. Happy have I been here, and I do not forget that you saved me from the wicked king and his son. But I must go home."

"Well spoken!" cried the bird. "I would not have had you choose otherwise! A father's grief, and the love of a brave knight which has brought him through ice and fire to find you are greater claims than mine!"

They feasted that night at the golden castle, and the next day the Ailpein bird took them on his back and flew with them to the edge of the kingdoms of the world, and there he set them down.

"Farewell," said the Ailpein bird. "But we shall meet again!"

As they had left the white wain behind in the kingdom of the birds, the knight found horses for them in the first town they came to.

Then he and the princess rode back, into one kingdom and out of it, into another and so on and on, until they came to the wicked king's. The princess was afraid to go through the land, but she need not have had any fear, for when they got to the place where the castle had stood there was not a stone left standing of it, for the princess' father and his army had pulled it down and the wicked king and his son were dead.

When they got home at last the king was beside himself with joy, at having his daughter safe home again. So what else could he do but give the brave knight his daughter's hand in marriage—if she was willing, that is, and you may be sure she was.

When they told the tale of their adventures everyone who heard marveled. The harper made a story of it to tell at the wedding, and that's the story that you have just heard.

Everyone in the kingdom, great and small, came to see the princess married to the brave young knight. The old woman who had given him the three feathers dressed the princess in her bridal gown, and proud she was to be the one who did it.

After they were married, while they sat at the wedding feast, three birds flew in through the window. But nobody even thought of bad luck, for they all had heard the harper's tale, so they knew who the birds were. The birds flew down and struck their beaks thrice on the floor and their feathers fell away. Then out stepped three fine young men. One had red-gold hair, and one had hair as black as the night, but the third one they had never seen before, and that one had hair as yellow as his own golden castle and he was the king of the birds.

The wedding feast lasted for a week, and then everyone went home. The three birds took on their feathers, but they did not say good-by. "We shall meet again!" cried they, as they flew away into the sky—and so they all did, and many and many a time.

So the king had his daughter back, and the brave knight had his princess, and she had the knight, and all of them were happy all the rest of their days.

The Woman Who Flummoxed
the Fairies

THERE WAS A WOMAN ONCE who was a master baker. Her bannocks were like wheaten cakes, her wheaten cakes were like the finest pastries, and her pastries were like nothing but Heaven itself in the mouth!

Not having her match, or anything like it, in seven counties round she made a good penny by it, for there wasn't a wedding nor a christening for miles around in the countryside but she was called upon to make the cakes for it, and she got all the trade of all the gentry as well. She was fair in her prices and she was honest, too, but she was that goodhearted into the bargain. Those who could pay well she charged aplenty, but when some poor body came and begged her to make a wee bit of a cake for a celebration and timidly offered her the little money they had for it, she'd wave it away and tell them to pay her when they got the cake. Then she'd set to and bake a cake as fine and big as any she'd make for a laird, and she'd send it to them as a gift, with the best respects of her husband and herself, to the wedding pair or the parents of the baby that was to be christened, so nobody's feelings were hurt.

Not only was she a master baker, but she was the cleverest

woman in the world; and it was the first that got her into trouble, but it was the second that got her out of it.

The fairies have their own good foods to eat, but they dearly love a bit of baker's cake once in a while, and will often steal a slice of one by night from a kitchen while all the folks in a house are sleeping.

In a nearby hill there was a place where the fairies lived, and of all cakes the ones the fairies liked best were the ones this master baker made. The trouble was, the taste of one was hard to come by, for her cakes were all so good that they were always eaten up at a sitting, with hardly a crumb left over for a poor fairy to find.

So then the fairies plotted together to carry the woman away and to keep her with them always just to bake cakes for them.

Their chance came not long after, for there was to be a great wedding at the castle with hundreds of guests invited, and the woman was to make the cakes. There would have to be so many of them, with so many people coming to eat them, that the woman was to spend the whole day before the wedding in the castle kitchen doing nothing but bake one cake after another!

The fairies learned about this from one of their number who had been listening at the keyhole of the baker's door. They found out, too, what road she'd be taking coming home.

When the night came, there they were by a fairy mound where the road went by, hiding in flower cups, and under leaves, and in all manner of places.

When she came by they all flew out at her. "The fireflies are gey thick the night," said she. But it was not fireflies. It was fairies with the moonlight sparkling on their wings.

Then the fairies drifted fern seed into her eyes, and all of a sudden she was that sleepy that she could go not one step farther without a bit of a rest!

"Mercy me!" she said with a yawn. "It's worn myself out I have this day!" And she sank down on what she took to be a grassy bank to doze just for a minute. But it wasn't a bank at all. It was the fairy mound, and once she lay upon it she was in the fairies' power.

She knew nothing about that nor anything else till she woke again, and found herself in fairyland. Being a clever woman she didn't have to be told where she was, and she guessed how she got there. But she didn't let on.

"Well now," she said happily, "and did you ever! It's all my life I've wanted to get a peep into fairyland. And here I am!"

They told her what they wanted, and she said to herself, indeed she had no notion of staying there the rest of her life! But she didn't tell the fairies that either.

"To be sure!" she said cheerfully. "Why you poor wee things! To think of me baking cakes for everyone else, and not a one for you! So let's be at it," said she, "with no time wasted."

Then from her kittiebag that hung at her side she took a clean apron and tied it around her waist, while the fairies, happy that she was so willing, licked their lips in anticipation and rubbed their hands for joy.

"Let me see now," said she, looking about her. "Well, 'tis plain you have nothing for me to be baking a cake with. You'll just have to be going to my own kitchen to fetch back what I'll need."

Yes, the fairies could do that. So she sent some for eggs, and some for sugar, and some for flour, and some for butter, while others flew off to get a wheen of other things she told them she had to have. At last all was ready for the mixing and the woman asked for a bowl. But the biggest one they could find for her was the size of a teacup, and a wee dainty one at that.

Well then, there was nothing for it, but they must go and fetch her big yellow crockery bowl from off the shelf over the water butt. And after that it was her wooden spoons and her egg whisp and one thing and another, till the fairies were all fagged out, what with the flying back and forth, and the carrying, and only the thought of the cake to come of it kept their spirits up at all.

At last everything she wanted was at hand. The woman began to measure and mix and whip and beat. But all of a sudden she stopped.

" 'Tis no use!" she sighed. "I can't ever seem to mix a cake without my cat beside me, purring."

"Fetch the cat!" said the fairy king sharply.

So they fetched the cat. The cat lay at the woman's feet and purred, and the woman stirred away at the bowl, and for a while all was well. But not for long.

The woman let go of the spoon and sighed again. "Well now, would you think it?" said she. "I'm that used to my dog setting the time of my beating by the way he snores at every second beat that I can't seem to get the beat right without him."

"Fetch the dog!" cried the king.

So they fetched the dog and he curled up at her feet beside the cat. The dog snored, the cat purred, the woman beat the cake batter, and all was well again. Or so the fairies thought.

But no! The woman stopped again. "I'm that worrited about my babe," said she. "Away from him all night as I've been, and him with a new tooth pushing through this very week. It seems I just can't mix . . ."

38

"Fetch that babe!" roared the fairy king, without waiting for her to finish what she was saying. And they fetched the babe.

So the woman began to beat the batter again. But when they brought the babe, he began to scream the minute he saw her, for he was hungry, as she knew he would be, because he never would let his dadda feed him his porridge and she had not been home to do it.

"I'm sorry to trouble you," said the woman, raising her voice above the screaming of the babe, "but I can't stop beating now lest the cake go wrong. Happen my husband could get the babe quiet if . . ."

The fairies didn't wait for the king to tell them what to do. Off they flew and fetched the husband back with them. He, poor man, was all in a whirl, what with things disappearing from under his eyes right and left, and then being snatched through the air himself the way he was. But here was his wife, and he knew where she was things couldn't go far wrong. But the baby went on screaming.

So the woman beat the batter, and the baby screamed, and the cat purred, and the dog snored, and the man rubbed his eyes and watched his wife to see what she was up to. The fairies settled down, though 'twas plain to see that the babe's screaming disturbed them. Still, they looked hopeful.

Then the woman reached over and took up the egg whisp and gave the wooden spoon to the babe, who at once began to bang away with it, screaming just the same. Under cover of the screaming of the babe and the banging of the spoon and the swishing of the egg whisp the woman whispered to her husband, "Pinch the dog!"

"What?" said the man. But he did it just the same—and kept on doing it.

"Tow! ROW! ROW!" barked the dog, and added his voice to the babe's screams, and the banging of the wooden spoon, and the swishing of the egg whisp.

"Tread on the tail of the cat!" whispered the woman to her husband, and it's a wonder he could hear her. But he did. He had got the notion now and he entered the game for himself. He not only trod on the tail of the cat, but he kept his foot there while the cat howled like a dozen lost souls.

So the woman swished, and the baby screamed, and the wooden spoon banged, and the dog yelped, and the cat howled, and the whole of it made a terrible din. The fairies, king and all, flew round and round in distraction with their hands over their ears, for if there is one thing the fairies can't bear it's a lot of noise and there was a lot more than a lot of noise in fairyland that day! And what's more the woman knew what they liked and what they didn't all the time!

So then the woman got up and poured the batter into two pans that stood ready. She laid by the egg whisp and took the wooden spoon away from the babe, and picking him up she popped a lump of sugar into his mouth. That surprised him so much that he stopped screaming. She nodded to her husband and he stopped pinching the dog and took his foot from the cat's tail, and in a minute's time all was quiet. The fairies stopped flying round and round and sank down exhausted.

And then the woman said, "The cake's ready for the baking. Where's the oven?"

The fairies looked at each other in dismay, and at last the fairy queen said weakly, "There isn't any oven."

"What!" exclaimed the woman. "No oven? Well then, how do you expect me to be baking the cake?"

None of the fairies could find the answer to that.

41

"Well then," said the woman, "you'll just have to be taking me and the cake home to bake it in my own oven, and bring me back later when the cake's all done."

The fairies looked at the babe and the wooden spoon and the egg whisp and the dog and the cat and the man. And then they all shuddered like one.

"You may all go!" said the fairy king. "But don't ask us to be taking you. We're all too tired."

"Och, you must have your cake then," said the woman, feeling sorry for them now she'd got what she wanted, which was to go back to her own home, "after all the trouble you've had for it! I'll tell you what I'll do. After it's baked, I'll be leaving it for you beside the road, behind the bank where you found me. And what's more I'll put one there for you every single week's end from now on."

The thought of having one of the woman's cakes every week revived the fairies so that they forgot they were all worn out. Or almost did.

"I'll not be outdone!" cried the fairy king. "For what you find in that same place shall be your own!"

Then the woman picked up the pans of batter, and the man tucked the bowls and spoons and things under one arm and the baby under the other. The fairy king raised an arm and the hill split open. Out they all walked, the woman with the pans of batter, the man with the bowls and the babe, and the dog and the cat at their heels. Down the road they walked and back to their own house, and never looked behind them.

When they got back to their home the woman put the pans of batter into the oven, and then she dished out the porridge that stood keeping hot on the back of the fire and gave the babe his supper.

There wasn't a sound in that house except for the clock ticking and the kettle singing and the cat purring and the dog snoring. And all those were soft, quiet sounds.

"I'll tell you what," said the man at last. "It doesn't seem fair on the rest of the men that I should have the master baker and the cleverest woman in the world all in one wife."

"Trade me off then for one of the ordinary kind," said his wife, laughing at him.

"I'll not do it," said he. "I'm very well suited as I am."

So that's the way the woman flummoxed the fairies. A good thing she made out of it, too, for when the cake was baked and cooled the woman took it up and put it behind the fairy mound, as she had promised. And when she set it down she saw there a little brown bag. She took the bag up and opened it and looked within, and it was full of bright shining yellow gold pieces.

And so it went, week after week. A cake for the fairies, a bag of gold for the woman and her husband. They never saw one of the fairies again, but the bargain never was broken and they grew rich by it. So of course they lived, as why should they not, happily ever after.

The Lairdie with the Heart of Gold

THERE ONCE WAS a young Scottish lairdie that folks all said had a heart of gold. That was because he could not bear the sight of anybody in trouble without trying to do something to help them. He was that good-natured and open-handed, his like would be hard to find.

He was a wee lad when his mother died, and his father, the old laird, never got over her death. He sent the laddie to live with a connection of the family in the North country, for the son took after the mother so much that the old laird could not look upon his face without sorrow.

Well, the lad grew up, and by-and-by the old laird died, so they sent for the young lairdie to come back and take over the estates. When he did he was sorry he'd come, for the old laird had let everything go to rack and ruin whilst he shut himself up into his study and read his books and broke his heart over losing his wife.

When the notary read out the list of what was coming to the young laird it sounded grand enough. There was a lot of land, and a village with a kirk, and some farms here and there, and a grand park with deer in it. And, of course, there was the castle.

But when the lairdie rode about looking at what his father had left him, there was another side to the story. The land was there, right enough, but most of it had gone wild. Only two or three of the farms were being kept up proper, and the rest weren't worth the name. Most of the houses in the village were tumble-down, and as for the kirk, it looked noble enough outside, but inside it was fitter to use for a barn than to worship and it had a big hole in the roof. The deer in the park were the only things that the lairdie took any comfort in, for they were sleek and friendly, and nothing else he'd seen that day, human or not, had been either the one or the other.

And when he got back to the castle and gave it a good look over, he saw that it was as bad as all the rest. The only thing good about it was the old family servants, who loved him and tried to make him comfortable.

But it wasn't much wonder he wished he'd stayed away.

Well, half a dozen years went by, and things were no worse, for they couldn't be, but certainly little better. Every quarter day, when rents were due, 'twas always the same. Some of the tenants were honest, but couldn't pay because they had had ill luck. And some of them who were able to pay were dishonest, and put on a meeching look and pretended they didn't have any money either. Only the two or three good farmers paid up regularly and in full. So what the lairdie collected was hardly more than enough to keep bannocks and cheese on the table. But the lairdie was so goodhearted that he believed them all, and felt sorry for them.

He might have had more for himself if he'd turned the servants off, but they were all getting along in years and he was afraid they'd never find new places. Besides, he loved them and they loved him, although about all they got out of it was a roof over their heads and as good to eat as he got—which wasn't any too much. There was a mortal lot of them, so the young laird worrited himself a good bit about how he'd take care of them all.

One winter's quarter day the lairdie came back in the gloaming from gathering rents all day, which was something he had to do himself, for if he had waited for them to be brought to him he'd have had a long, long wait. All he had got was excuses and promises, with barely enough money to tide him over until the next quarter day. He was that disheartened that he didn't know what to do. He'd left his horse at home because he didn't like to take the poor beast out all day in the bad wintry weather, so he plodded along on foot in the dusk with his head down against the snow and the wind.

There was a fork in the road where half of it went down to the mill beyond and the other half went up the hill to the castle. There at the place where the roads parted he saw what he took to be a heap of bairns' toys by the roadside, with a lot of poppets beside them. He couldn't see so well with the dark closing in, but when he got up to them he gave them another look. Then he saw the pile wasn't toys at all! Nor were the other things poppets, for they were all as alive and breathing as he was himself!

It was a whole lot of brownies, and the heap of things were their wee sticks of furniture.

"Well!" exclaimed the lairdie. "What is it you're doing here, out in the wind and the snow and the cold?"

Then one of the brownies stepped out from the rest. "I'm Lachie Tosh," said he, "and this is my wife and our seven sons

47

and their wives, with each their seven sons and their sons'
wives and their bairns and all. I'm the head of our *sept* of our
clan," said he, "and we're flitting."

The lairdie bent down and politely took the hand the wee
man offered him.

"Where are you flitting to?" he asked.

"We're flitting from the mill," Lachie Tosh told him, "and
it's bitter hard that we should be made to. The Toshes have
always lived at the mill since time began. My father, and his
father, and his father's father, and all our fathers before them
have been mill brownies. But the miller's wife died, and now
he has brought a new wife from the town and she'll have
naught to do with the brownies!"

"She says there are no brownies!" cried one of the clan.

"She says we are just great brown rats!" shrieked another.

Then they all began shouting at one and the same time.

"She says that we steal the meal!"

"That we nibble holes in the cheese!"

"That we take the eggs from the nests!"

"That we skim the cream from the milk!"

"She brought in a great cruel cat to fright our bairns!"

"And two fierce dogs to chase us away from the corn!"

"Whisht!" shouted Lachie Tosh and he held up a hand.
At once the babble stopped. "So that's why we're flitting,"
said the brownie.

"Och aye!" said the lairdie. "I can see that well. But where
will you be going now?"

"Well," said Lachie Tosh, "that's what we're doing here.
We stopped to talk it over. But they've all been havering for
an hour gone, and not yet picked a place."

The laird was sore troubled by the brownies' plight. "The
castle has little to offer you," he said, "but you'd be warm and

dry there anyway. The servants are an old-fashioned sort and I doubt not you'd be welcome. The cook has a cat, 'tis true, but she's a comfortable, purring sort of a beastie and doesn't even trouble the mice. As for my two dogs, they would be no trouble to you, for they are that friendly they sport about the garden with the hares and do them no harm at all. Would you like to come with me to the castle?"

"Aye, that would we!" said Lachie Tosh.

But the lairdie thought he'd best give them a word of warning. "You'll find we have not much to do with, but what we have we'll gladly share. There'll be porridge and milk, and happen a bannock and some cheese, too. Whatever there is you're welcome to it."

"Say no more!" cried Lachie Tosh. "Come all!"

The brownie men picked up their wee bits of furniture, and the brownie women took up their bundles and some of their smaller bairns, and up they all trooped after the laird to the castle.

The housekeeper met them in the hall, for she had been keeping an eye out for the lairdie. What with the dark coming on and him out so late she was near troubled to death.

When he opened the door and led the brownie folk in, she stood, dumbstruck, in her tracks.

"Mistress MacIvor," the lairdie said to her, "I've brought you the brownie o' the mill. They've been turned out by the miller's new, townbred wife, and have no place to shelter themselves in."

The housekeeper found her tongue at that. "Och, the poor wee things!" she cried. "Come in! Come in all! Come in to the fire and give yourselves a warming."

"Will ye have room for us all?" asked Lachie Tosh. "We're wee, but there's awful many of us."

49

"Is it room, he asks?" demanded the housekeeper. "In this great place, with the few of us rattling about in it? Och, you'll be doing us a favor, helping to fill it up so it don't feel so empty-like!"

Lachie Tosh was well pleased with that and said so gratefully, and in no time at all the brownies were settled into the castle as if they'd always been there.

The cat and the dogs made no trouble at all. Indeed the cat seemed to think that the brownie weans were kittens of a sort, for she cuddled them and washed their faces and hands and purred them to sleep before the fire. As for the laird's dogs, they acted as if their lives had ne'er been complete till the brownies came.

The servants liked the brownies' cheerful chatter and their pleasant faces, and on the whole it was agreed that the castle was a better place since the brownies came. The candles burned brighter, the fires blazed higher and took less fuel to do it. The hens laid more eggs, the meal sack seemed to grow heavier instead of lighter each day, and there was more cream to the milk the cows gave. There seemed to be more food for the table instead of less, with all the extra mouths to be filled, so all were contented.

But no, not all. Lachie Tosh would go out every morn and be gone for a long time. When he came back the frown on his brow reached down to his rosy old cheeks and the corners of his mouth drooped down farther each day. And as for the laird, his nice young face grew longer and sadder day by day.

When the brownies had been in the castle a little above a month the lairdie sat in his study one day over his account books. The study was a cheerful place now, for the brownie women had everything as neat as a silver pin, and a big fire burned in the fireplace. But the laird's face was far from cheerful because he was trying to balance his accounts, and with so much paid out and so little paid in he couldn't do it.

Lachie Tosh came in and climbed up into a chair facing the laird. The laird laid his pen down, for he saw the brownie had come to talk to him.

"Lairdie," said the brownie. "I've something to say that happen you won't be liking."

"Och, Lachie," the laird said, "there's naught you could say I'd take amiss."

"Well, 'tis my way to speak plain, so speak plain I will!" said Lachie. "I do not like the way things is going on here."

"That is what I feared," the laird said sadly. "And now you'll be wanting to go away no doubt? Well, the castle is but a poor place and I cannot say I blame you. But it's glad we've been to have you all here, and we'll all be sorry to see you go."

"Och, nay!" said the brownie indignantly. "You've read my meaning wrong! We're all as snug here as e'er we could hope to be. We're the castle brownies now! We're settled here to stay."

"I'm happy to hear it," said the laird with relief.

"It's things outside the castle is wrong," said the Lachie earnestly. " 'Willful waste makes woeful want.' That's where the trouble lies, lairdie!"

"I know it," said the laird. "I know it well."

"And another thing," said Lachie, "butter and brawn in the cottage and bannocks and cheese in the castle is not right and never will be!"

"But how can the cottagers have butter and meat when they can't even pay their rents? There aren't many of them who can find money for things like that."

"More than you know!" said Lachie.

51

"But how would they come by the money?" the laird insisted. "They've told me often that they can't make ends meet."

"They get the money by not paying their rent," said Lachie. "That's how!"

The laird looked at Lachie Tosh, and Lachie looked right back at him.

"I've been going round and about," said Lachie. "A wee person like me sees more than sees him. I know who has money laid by that hasn't paid their rent since the old laird's time. And the laziness and thriftlessness and shiftlessness I've seen makes the blood of me boil with rage. I'd best say no more about it!"

"No doubt you're right, Lachie," said the laird. "But what am I to do? I've thought till my head swims and I can't find a way to set things right."

"It's the heart of gold of you," said Lachie gently. "You trust everybody and you believe every tale they tell you. You're too good to folks. Lairdie, what you need is a factor!"

"I'd have one if I could pay him," said the laird. "Someone who knows how to go about managing an estate would do much better than me. And well do I know it! How could I ever pay a factor?"

"How about me?" asked Lachie. "I'll take it on if you like."

The laird sat up in his chair and stared at the brownie. "You, Lachie!" he exclaimed.

"Why not me?" asked Lachie. "Me and the help I'd get from my sons, and my son's sons and the rest. 'Twould take a sharp rascal to be getting the better of all of us. 'Twould now!"

The laird looked troubled. "I wouldn't want you to be hard

on the folks whose luck has been lacking," he said doubt-fully.

"Those that deserve good will get it," said Lachie firmly, "and those that don't, won't. And you need not fear I'd be mistaking the one for the other, either."

"I just don't know," said the lairdie.

"I might even find ways of mending the luck of those who need it," said Lachie slyly. That brought the laird over, as Lachie knew it would.

"Well," said the laird, "you might have a try at it, Lachie, if you like."

"Give me the books, then," Lachie ordered, "and go to bed, and leave me to get on with it."

The laird gave the brownie his books and off he went to bed. Strangely, he slept sound that night. 'Twas the first time he'd done so since he came back to the castle.

The brownie got no sleep at all, for he sat all night over the books, and what he learned about the way the tenants paid—or didn't pay—made him pound the pages with his wee fists and grin with rage!

Folks found things weren't the same as they used to be when Lachie Tosh took over!

The letters were the start of it. They began to fall like big flakes of snow, thick and fast. Those that got them didn't fancy them much. They were all written in a very small crabbed script, and they were short and very plain-spoken. All of them told folks what they hadn't done, and to do it at once and no excuses accepted!

"Your fence wants mending. Tend to it!" said one letter.

Another one read, "Give your shed a wash of white. Your cow is ashamed to bide in it."

"You've twenty pounds of silver in the box hidden under

your bed, that you're owing to the laird. See that he gets it," another letter said; and still another, "If you'd rather eat well than pay your rent go do it elsewhere."

There were more of them, and all of them were the unpleasant sort, like the ones you've heard about. All were signed "Lachie Tosh, Factor."

Folks went around asking each other, "Who *is* this Lachie Tosh?" Not a soul could answer that, but it was uncanny the way he knew all the secrets anyone had. He knew everything, and he let folks know he knew, and what he knew. The lazy ones, the thriftless ones, the dishonest ones had no peace at all! For whoever he was or wherever he came from, it was sure he had a terrible rough tongue—in his letters. But nobody ever got the bit of a sight of him.

It was no use to rush to the castle and demand that he come forth. All they saw was the housekeeper, who gave them the sort of a welcome that sent them hurrying back home, wishing they hadn't come. And it was no use taking their troubles to the laird, for although he listened politely all he said at the end was, "You'll have to take it up with the factor."

So they all soon learned it saved them trouble to do what they were told and no fuss about it. As for those who were too lazy to mend their ways they were told to pack up their families and go. And they did that, and a good riddance it was.

Och aye! The good times was over, for the lairdie had got him a factor!

It was wonderful the way things got better. Farms looked like farms and as if farmers had the lease of them. The church roof got mended and so did the houses along the village street.

It was a wonder to see, too, how things picked up for those

whose luck wanted mending. This one got health, that had lacked it for a year. Another one's lad heard of a place in town needing a young fellow, and went and got took on. The oldest lass of a widow had a chance to go into service where she was happy and well paid. So both of them were able to send money to help out at home. Little by little the ill luck went away, and none of the folks on the laird's estate remembered it any more.

When the next quarter day come around it was a treat to see folks coming up to the castle to pay what they owed. When it was over Lachie Tosh came out of the cupboard where he'd been hiding to keep an eye on them all and make sure all paid up as they should.

He came out, rubbing his wee hands together in glee. "Well," said he, "the accounts is balanced now with plenty over to spare. So now we'd better take heed to yourself, lairdie."

"There's nothing I need," said the laird. " 'Tis yourself should have something, Lachie, for all of the toil and trouble has been yours."

"Och! You and your heart of gold!" scolded Lachie. "With all of us living off you now, from me down to the least bairn of my sons' sons' sons! Let us have no more foolish talk!"

And then the brownie added, "There's two things you need, and the first one's clothes. You're that threadbare I'm ashamed to see you walking out, lest the clothes on your back leave you entirely. So off you go to town to have the tailor make you a fine suit of clothes, and when you come back I'll tell you what is the other thing you need."

So the lairdie went off to town, since Lachie said he had to. In a week's time he came back dressed in his fine new clothes, and there wasn't a lad to match him in looks in all of Scotland.

Lachie looked him over before and behind and up and down.

"Ye'll do!" said Lachie. "And now for the second thing you need. And that's a wife!"

"A wife!" said the laird. He sounded scared, but you could tell he was a bit pleased at the notion, too. "But where will I be finding one?"

"Look about till you do!" Lachie told him.

"I've ne'er had o'ermuch to do with lassies. What would I be saying to her?" asked the poor lairdie.

"Och, you could ask her what she'd be thinking of brownies in the house," said Lachie.

"Aye. I could do that," the laird said. "But look now, Lachie! How will I know she's the right one?"

"Do not trouble yourself about that. You'll know right enough, when the time comes," Lachie said, "and there'll be no way to mistake her."

So the lairdie rode away to the North, where he had a cousin living. He met a likely lass there, and when he had a chance to get her alone he asked her, "What do you think of brownies?"

She looked at him, surprised-like, and said in her plain North country way, "Brownies? Och, I dinna think o' them at all! Because I dinna believe in 'em."

Well, to be sure she wasn't the one he wanted! So he went away from there.

Then he rode to the South, and there he met as fine a lass as he had ever seen, just back from a Lady School in Edinboro'. She was not only handsome, but terribly well learned, too. So, after they got better acquainted he asked her, "What would your opinion be of brownies in the house?"

"My good man," said she in her fancy Lady School voice, "the idea of the existence of brownies is the attempt of the

57

common people to explain the disappearance of the ancient Picts!"

The lairdie got away from there in a hurry! Whew! **That** one would never do at all!

He had another cousin living in the East, so he rode over there. He liked the looks of a lass he found in his cousin's house, for she was a bonnie wee thing, not much bigger than a brownie herself. He soon got friendly with her, so one evening he asked her, "What would you be thinking of a brownie in the house?"

At that she threw up her hands and screamed! "Oh!" she cried. "I couldn't bear the thought of it! The horrid little things! And in the house! Oh no!"

Well, the lairdie wouldn't want that one and no mistake about it!

And now there was no place to ride to, except to the West. But he fared no better there. For when he asked his question of a lass he found there, she said, "I've never given it a thought, but I'm fair certain I'd not be liking them at all."

So there he was, with nothing to do but ride home and tell Lachie he couldn't find the right lass, North, South, East, or West.

As he was riding home he came by the mill the brownies had flitted from. There, on a bench by the door of the mill, sat a bonnie lass with her hands in her lap. It was the miller's daughter, and she was feeling sad, for she and the wife her father had brought from town didn't get on well, having different notions about almost everything.

When the lairdie saw her, his heart gave a jump for here was a lass he could fancy! So he stopped his horse, and gave her a good day.

She looked up at him, and he looked down at her, and he asked her, "What do you think of brownies in the house?"

She had been weeping and there were tears in her eyes, but she smiled through the tears and she said, "Och the dear wee things! There were always brownies at the mill when my mother was alive!"

So he took her up on his horse with him and off he rode to the castle, to tell Lachie he'd found the lass he wanted for his wife.

Lachie looked at her and he looked at the laird and he smiled all over his face.

"You went too far afield, my lad," said he. "I could have told you so. She's the one I was thinking of when I told you to look about!"

So the laird married the miller's daughter, and it was a grand big wedding. All the brownies, from Lachie to the least one, came to it, too, for the lairdie and the miller's daughter said there'd be no wedding at all unless the brownies were there. It was strange that none of the other guests noticed them, but it must have been because they were enjoying themselves too much to pay any heed to the wee folks!

And ever after all went well, and why should aught go wrong, with the castle full of brownies, and Lachie Tosh for the factor, and a lass who loved the brownies, and a laird with a heart of gold!

The Gay Goss-Hawk

THERE WAS ONCE a young English lady of very high degree. She had a father and seven brothers and a stepmother whom her father had married but lately. The father and her seven brothers loved her well enough, but the stepmother had no liking for her, being envious because the lady was young and good and beautiful, and the stepmother was none of the three. So the poor young English lady was not happy at home, for her stepmother lost no chance of making sure that she wouldn't be.

Well there came a time when the English king called together all his court, and the young lady was there, too, with all her family. And there she met a gay Scottish laird, who was so gentle and kind that she loved him without half trying and he loved her the same.

Well since she loved him and he loved her they plighted their troth and promised to wed. As a pledge of love he gave her the gold ring from his finger, and she gave him a blue silken bow from her dress, tied in a true love knot.

The Scottish laird went to her father to ask for the lady's hand in marriage. But the father wouldn't have it at all, for he and her seven brothers had planned to marry her off to an old English lord who was very wealthy, and who also had the ear of the English king ready to listen to whatever he liked to say.

The Scottish laird had plenty of gold and a house and land. He had a thousand good men of his clan to serve him in his need. But the lady's father scorned the Scots, as a proud, wild, stiff-necked race, and he told the laird he'd have none of him to be his son-in-law.

Then the stepmother said the lovers would be meeting, since they were at the king's court together, so to prevent it her father carried her off to his own castle far away. After she had gone, the Scottish laird had no pleasure at the king's court, so he packed up and went back to his own castle in the North country.

The only thing that pleased him there was a gay goss-hawk that he had. He soon grew fond of it, for it sang to him merrily when he was sad. And it went with him wherever he went and was his faithful companion. It would perch on his knee when he sat, or sit by his plate when he ate, or ride on his wrist as he went about his lands. It was a very intelligent bird, and had learned to know the laird so well that it understood all that he said to it.

But nothing could comfort the laird for the loss of his love. He grew as wan and pale in his castle as the lady did in hers.

At last the laird sat down and wrote a letter to his love, and in it, he told her to come to him soon or he would surely die. He told the goss-hawk that he must carry the letter to England and give it to the young English lady.

"Though you've never laid eyes upon her," he said to the goss-hawk, "you'll know her from all the rest, for she is the fairest lady of all in the length and breadth of the land."

Then the laird told the bird the way he was to go, to find the lady's father's castle. When the goss-hawk got there he was to sit in the birch tree that stood by the door of the lady's bower, and when the lady came out with her maidens to go to church then he should sing so that the lady would notice him. If she stopped and came to the tree the goss-hawk could give her the letter.

The laird hung the true love knot the lady had given him about the goss-hawk's neck, so she'd know who was sending him to her.

The bird took the letter in its beak and stretched its wings out wide, and off it flew to the English castle.

When the goss-hawk came to the castle of the English lady's father he sat himself down upon a branch of the birch tree by the lady's bower that the laird had told him about. The letter he tucked under his wing to hide it away. By-and-by out comes the lady to church and all her maidens along with her. Right merrily did the goss-hawk sing, then, and the lady turned her head and looked back at him. When she saw the blue true love's knot about the bird's neck she knew who had sent him there, so she told her maidens to be walking on and she'd come to them a little later. So off they went without her and never turned to look back at her.

Back she went to the gay goss-hawk and bade him sing again. And first he sang a merry song and then he sang a sad one, and then he took the letter from under his wing and gave it to the fair English lady, for he knew that she was the one his master had told him about.

The lady unfolded the letter and began to read it. First she turned pale as a white rose and then she turned rosy as a red one, and when she finished she read it all again.

She wrote a letter to tell the laird to bake his bridal bread and to brew his bridal ale, because before either of them had a chance to grow stale she'd be at St. Mary's church to meet him.

The goss-hawk took the letter and off and away he flew, and he never stopped for bite nor for sup till he'd laid the letter safe in the hand of the young Scottish laird.

When the bird was gone the lady sat long, to think what she was to do. Then she rose and went up to her bedchamber and laid herself down on her bed. Her maidens came seeking her, for it troubled them that she had not come to them at the church, and they found her lying there.

"Go fetch my father quickly," she said, "for I feel ill and I think I'm about to die!"

The maidens ran for her father and told them what she had said. He came and stood at her bedside, and she looked at him. "Father," said she, "before I die will you grant one wish to me?"

"Do not ask for your Scottish laird," her father said with a frown. "Anything else I will promise to you, whatever it may be. But rather than see you wedded to yon proud Scottish laird I'd see you lying dead!"

"Well then," said the lady, "should I die, will you give me your promise true that my seven brothers shall carry me to Scotland to be buried? And when they come to the first church there let them stop and have the Mass sung over me. And when they come to the second church let them have the church bells tolled for me. But when they come to St. Mary's church, they must set me down in the churchyard and wait there till the night."

Her father promised all that she asked, and then he went away. In the dead of the night, when all in the castle were asleep and her old nurse dozing by the fire, the lady got up

from her bed. She mixed herself a sleeping draught, and when it was mixed she drank it down, and then she slipped back into her bed.

At dawn of day the old nurse awoke, and there was her fair young lady lying so still and white that anyone would be sure she was dead. She roused all the castle and told them that the lady had died in her sleep. Her father came and her seven brothers came, and they all stood grieving about the lady's bed. Then came her stepmother and stood looking at her. "We'll make sure she is dead then," said the stepmother.

First she sent for a sharp silver pin, and when it was brought to her, she took it in her hand and stuck it into the lady's white arm. But the lady never blinked nor moved at all when the pin went in. Then the stepmother sent for a pan of hot, boiling wax, and when it came she dropped three drops of it upon the lady's white, white breast. But the lady did not sigh, nor did she flinch, but she lay there with no sign of life.

Then her seven brothers made a bier, and they made it all of oaken boughs. They covered it over with silver cloth, as was fitting for a lady of such high degree.

Her maidens took white velvet and made her a white velvet cap and a white velvet coverlet for her bier, and with every stitch they took, they sewed on a little silver bell.

When all was ready her maidens washed and dressed her, and they combed her long golden hair. They took her from her bed and they laid her on the silver bier, and upon her head they set the velvet cap, and they lay the velvet coverlet over her.

Then her seven brothers took up the bier, and all the little silver bells rang sweetly as they carried her away to Scotland.

When they came to the first church the seven brothers set the bier down, and there they had the Mass sung over her. At the second church they stopped again, and there her seven brothers had the church bells rung for her.

But the third Scottish church was St. Mary's church. The seven brothers carried the bier into the churchyard, for there they were to wait until the night. But when they came in up sprang a hundred spearmen, and out from the midst of them stepped the young Scottish laird. He bade the seven brothers to set down the lady's bier, that he might look upon her face. He took her by the hand and up she rose at once, and smiled upon him lovingly. She set herself among the spearmen, with her true love by her side, and the little silver bells upon her velvet cap chimed merrily together all the while.

"Go home! My seven brothers, go home!" she said, "for you've fetched me where I want to be!"

Then her seven brothers said, as they turned to go, "Shame to you that left your father to grieve at home because he thought you were dead!"

"Take my love to my father," she told them then, "though he said he'd rather I were lying dead than married to my Scottish laird. But I send no love to my cruel stepmother for the sharp silver pin she stuck me with and the hot, boiling wax she burned me with, for to her I wish nothing but woe!"

Then she rode off gaily beside her Scottish laird and the next day they were wed. And wherever they went, there went the goss-hawk, too, that had brought them together when they were parted. And happy they were, for all their troubles, like this story, had come to an end.

The Lass that Couldn't Be Frighted

THERE ONCE WAS A LASS and naught could ever give her a fright! At least, that was what folks said about her.

She lived all alone on a bit of a farm that stood in the forest. Her mother died when she was a wee thing, and her father—the poor man—was never much use to her, he being more often found at the inn, in the village nearby, than at home or at work. Besides that, one day he just wandered away somewhere, and wherever it was he went he never came back.

When it was plain to see he was gone for good folks told her she'd best come down to live in the village, seeing she had no kin of her own to take her in.

"But why should I?" she asked. "I'm very well as I am."

"Lawks!" said the folks. "And are you not afraid to bide by yourself in that lonesome place? 'Tis enough to fright the soul out of a body!"

"Think of all the wild beasts about!" they said.

"Hoots!" said she. "Well you know there are no wild beasts in the forest, barring a hart or happen a hare after the kail or a wee fox trying for the hen run."

But the cottagers were awful uneasy about her. For you

never could tell! The forest was big and dark. Anything could be in it—and there might be worse things abroad by night than wild beasties.

"What then?" she asked.

They looked to the left and they looked to the right, and then they put their heads close to hers and whispered, *"The Wee People!"*

"Och!" laughed she. "Goblins and ghaisties and such like! Goodwife's tales to scare the bairns with!"

They were horrified at that. Did she not believe in the Wee Folks? Well, she wouldn't say "aye," nor would she say "nay" to that. But what she did say was, that if there were any of them, why she didn't mind them at all.

So they gave up talking to her about it, but what they said to each other was that she was uncommon brave for a lassie. And that's how the story came about that she was a lassie that couldn't be frighted.

The strange thing was that it was true. With her dog and her cat she was well able to keep the hares from her garden and the foxes from her hens. And if a bear had come to rob her hives (though, of course, there were none in the forest) she'd just have twisted his ear and spatted him back to the forest with the flat of her hand to his backside. As for the fairies—well, if there were any about let them keep to their ways and she'd keep to hers.

With her house and her garden and her cow and her two sheep and her hens and her beehives she was well fixed, and with her dog and her cat for company what more could she ask?

True, she seldom saw money from one year's end to the other, but the things from her wee farm that she had over what she needed for her own use she could trade in at the shop in the village for whatever she couldn't raise or make for herself. So what good would money be to her, the way things were? And being contented, she was as happy as the day is long.

Then one day one of the lads from the village looked at her, and he saw that she was the bonniest lass in all the country-side. Then, having taken one look he took another, and saw that she had come to an age when she might well think of get-ting married. He went and told a friend or two and those took the word of it to one or two more, and in no time all the lads for miles around were clustered at her gate like bees in a swarm, all buzzing around at her to make her pick one of them to wed. All the lads but one, that is, and that one was Wully the weaver's son, who had a croft on the hillside over against the forest. When one of the lads told him she was awful bonny he said, aye he'd known that for long. And when they said she was old enough to wed he said that he knew that, too. And when they asked if he wasn't going to be woo-ing her the lads all thought he was plain daft, for he said, nay he thought he'd just bide his time, and up he climbed to his croft and tended his sheep.

Little good came to the ones who stayed to woo her, for she wouldn't have any of them.

"Why should I?" she asked them.

To protect her? Well, she hadn't had trouble doing that for herself. Besides, she had her dog.

For money? Well, that she did not want nor need.

For love? And she only laughed, and said that when the lad she could fancy came along she'd give that her considera-tion. But for the present, she'd stay as she was.

So at last all the lads were so discouraged that they left her to look elsewhere, which did not displease her at all.

71

The lads who had given up trying to win her told Wully the weaver's son that maybe he'd done well not to waste his time on such a headstrong lassie, and besides it wasn't natural for a lass not to be afraid of aught. But all Wully said was, "Och, we'll see then," and went on tending his sheep.

So days went by and weeks went by, and then one evening the lassie went to the meal bin to fetch herself some meal to make her some bannocks for supper.

"There now!" she said. "When I fill the bowl the bin will be empty!" and she scraped and scraped at the bottom of the bin. "There'll be no oatmeal for the porridge in the morn," said she.

So she made up her mind that as soon as she'd had her supper she'd take a sack of meal to have it ground at Hughie the miller's mill.

When she'd baked her bannocks and eaten them she went to the shed and filled a sack with oats, and taking it on her arm off she set for the mill. 'Twas a fine warm night, so she enjoyed the walk, but when she got to the mill the house beside it was dark and the mill shut tight, for the miller and all his family had gone off somewhere for a visit and there was nobody at home to grind her oats for her.

She set her sack on the sill of the house and sat herself down beside of it, to consider what she was to do.

Lachie the miller had a mill, too, but it lay over on the edge of the next village, a long ways off. It would be far to go, but she could think of nothing better to do if she was going to have porridge in the morning. So up she got and took up her bag of oats, and off she went again.

When she left Hughie's mill dusk was closing in, and when she got to Lachie's mill the night was as dark as the inside of one of the caves of Cruachan. Lachie's mill was idle and still and the door was locked, but that did not trouble her, for the house of the miller, over the way, showed a light. So she went up to the house and clackit at the door.

The miller came to the door and stood there staring at her.

"I've brought you a bag of oats to be ground at the mill," said the lass. And when the miller said nothing she added civilly, " 'Tis sorry I am to trouble you so late, but I've no meal in the house at all against the morn."

"I'll grind no meal in the mill tonight," said the miller then. "Come back on the morrow's morn."

But the lass wasn't going to be put off that way. "I'm telling you I've no meal in the house for the morning's porridge!" she said impatiently.

"Come back fasting then," said the miller, "for I'll grind no meal tonight!"

"Well then, give me the key to the mill," the lass told him, "and I'll grind my meal myself!"

"Woman!" roared the miller, "I will not grind your meal nor will I give you the key! For when anyone grinds grain in the mill o' nights a great ugly goblin comes up through the floor and steals the grain and beats him black and blue!"

"Hoots! Toots! to your goblin!" the lass shouted back at him. "I'll grind my grain, goblin or no goblin! *Miller, give me the key!*"

So determined was she that the miller fetched the key, but he would not give it to her until he had called his wife and all in his house to witness that he was not to blame whatever happened to her.

Then she took the key, and the miller's wife lit a lanthorn and gave it to her, to light her so that she could see to grind her meal.

The lass went off to the mill and unlocked the door. She

73

opened it and looked all about, but there was nothing there. So she went and opened the water into the race, and the mill wheel began to turn around. Clack! Clack! Whish! Clack! Clack! Whish! Clack! Clack! Whish! went the mill wheel.

So then she poured the grain into the hopper and sat herself down to rest a minute while the grain went through, for the long walk had tired her a little and she still had to walk back. But it was not long till the meal was through, so she let it pour out into her sack. When all her meal was in the sack she knotted the top, and she said to herself said she, "Well! There's nothing here to fash myself about!"

And just then up through the floor rose a great ugly goblin! He had a big black club in one hand and he stretched the other one out to grab her sack of meal!

"No you don't!" shrieked the lass, for the first thought in her mind was losing her morning's porridge. So she snatched the club from the goblin's hand and off she took after him.

Now the goblin had met many a man in that mill by night, but never before in all his days had he met a woman like the lass. He didn't know just what to do, for it was a new thing entirely, especially since she had hold of his club. A goblin's wits are never very fast at working so he just backed away.

The lass came after and banged the goblin over his ugly head with the big black club. Into the corners and out again she drove him, and round and round the mill, and sometimes she hit the goblin and sometimes she hit the wall, but all of it made a fearful sort of a racket.

The miller slammed the house door to and he and his wife and all they put their hands up over their ears to shut out the terrible din!

And then the goblin came up alongside the hopper where

75

the grain was poured down. Against the hopper there was a big oaken bar. The goblin just turned his back for a minute so as to take up the bar, and the lass came up close and planted her foot in the middle of the goblin's back and gave it a monstrous shove. Into the hopper headfirst went the goblin, and the lass turned the mill wheel on!

So there was the goblin between the mill stones, going round and round and round and round! It didn't kill him, for nothing can kill a goblin, but it hurt him awful bad.

"O-o-o-o-o-o-ow!" shrieked the goblin. "Let me out! Let me out! Let me out!" And he shrieked so loud it all but lifted the roof clear off of the mill. The miller and his wife and all were that frighted that they crept under their beds and pulled their pillows down tight over their ears. But even then they could hear the noise.

"Let me out!" screamed the goblin.

"Stay down there!" called the lass, as she wiped her face and settled her skirts, for the fight had been a hot one. " 'Twill do you good!"

"Och let me out," begged the goblin, "and I promise you I'll go away and bother you no more."

"You will, then?" asked the lass.

"I promise you I will," said the goblin.

"Well that's worth considering," said the lass.

She shut off the water. The mill wheel stopped turning, the goblin stopped screeching, and all was quiet. But the goblin didn't come up. So the lass reached down, and she caught hold of him by the neck, and she drew him up out of the hopper.

Never was there seen, since the beginning of time, such a terribly used-up goblin. He said not one word, but limped out through the door of the mill and never again was he seen or heard of in those parts.

The lass shouldered her sack of meal and took the goblin's club under her arm and the key and the lanthorn in her hand. She went out of the mill and locked the door and went across to the miller's house. She knocked on the door there for a long, long time before the miller got brave enough to open it. But at last he crept down the stairs and opened it a wee crack.

"Here's your lanthorn and here's your key," said the lass. "I've ground my meal and I've got rid of your goblin for you. And now I'm going home!" And home she did go, with the club and the sack of meal.

By the time she'd made her porridge in the morn the news was all over the village about how she'd driven the goblin out of Lachie's mill.

Lachie had risen early and told the tale all over the countryside. It was at the blacksmith's shop, where he'd stopped in to get a bit of mending done, that Wully the weaver's son heard about it. His heart ached inside of him, for he had been thinking that maybe the lass would change her mind someday about wanting a man to fend for her, and maybe if she did, he'd be that man. But that was when her being afraid of naught was just a lot of talk. But what he'd heard at the blacksmith shop looked like proof that the talk was true enough.

"Och," he said sadly, " 'tis sure she'll never be needing me now." He started up the road very slowly, one foot then t'other. But when he came where the road went into the forest, he heard something that made the hairs of his head stand straight up and he began to run. Because it was the lass's voice, and she was screaming at the top of it! Maybe it wasn't as loud as the goblin screamed, but it was close to that.

"It must be a band of robbers has got after her, and they're killing her," panted Wully, as he raced up the road toward her farm.

He came to her dooryard and rushed in, picking up a big club that lay by the gate as he ran.

He threw the door open and took a stand, ready to battle whoever was there, no matter how many! And then he stopped!

There was the lass, standing upon the table between the porridge bowl and the bowl of milk, holding her skirts to her knees and screaming for help with her eyes tight shut! And playing around on the floor below was a wee brown mousie.

Wully set the club down and leaned against the doorpost. He let her scream a little bit longer and then he said, "They've been telling me you're the lassie that nothing could fright."

The lass opened her eyes and cried to him, "Och Wully, put the beastie out! The dog's gone into the woods and the cat's off in the fields, and there's nobody here can save me but you!"

"Happen you need a man to take care of you after all," said Wully.

"Happen I do!" sighed the lass.

So he took the broom from behind the door, and he drove the wee beastie out of the house.

Then he jumped the lass down from the table, and took her in his arms and kissed her. "We'll be married o' Sunday," said Wully.

"Aye," said the lass, and she laid her head on his shoulder as if that was where it belonged.

So married they were, and happily, too. But whenever she

had a bit too much to say for herself, Wully would just say "mousie!" And then she'd grow rosy red and hang down her head, and have no more to say. With all so well understood between them 'tis no wonder that they lived happily ever after.

The Daughter of the King Ron

MANY A STRANGE TALE is told of the isles of the Gaelic seas, but surely none so strange as that of the daughter of the great King Ron.

How many of the isles there are would be hard to say, for the counting of them would be an endless task. Some of them are great islands, with harbors and towns and people upon them, but many of them have little soil and mostly rock, and on some of these no man ever sets his foot, for where would be the use of it?

Upon these small, deserted isles the Ron delights to dwell, for the rocks are grand places for him to be sunning himself, and in the pools and the little bays around them are the fish he likes best to eat. There, too, the rocks slant down into the water, and there the young seals sport and play, slipping down the smooth gray rocks and into the cool green water with never a splash.

Now some of the seals are not like other seals, for they can change their shapes if they will, and become men and women for as long as it pleases them. Fishermen tell tales of going out into the misty dawn and seeing the likes of a great man, strong and powerful, walking upon the rocks, or of coming in with their catch after sundown with night drawing in and hearing the voice of a woman singing a strange, wild, sweet song across the waters.

But never could a fisherman come close enough to get what would be a good look at whoever was there, for the hurling waves and the cruel rocks in the water about the islands made a wall to guard them, and where the gate of it would be nobody could know.

It is from these strange ones that the seals choose their kings. Now there was once a great King Ron who had many sons but only one daughter and she the least one of the family, and at the time the tale begins she was of little age, for her childhood had not long been left behind her.

The name of the king was Ailean Mor, which means Great Rock, and a great rock he was, to be sure, both in size and in strength. His daughter's name was Fionna, the Fair One, but her father had another name for her, for he called her Fear-charagh, the Best-Beloved. She was the apple of his eye and he kept her under that eye as best he could. But to be the King Ron has not the makings of an easy life, because the clans of the seals are many and spread over many seas, and each with its own chief, ruling in his own way. Often enough the Ron Mor had to be off and away, here and there, settling differences about fishing rights and such-like arguments. As he could not take his daughter with him, she just stayed at home.

Now across the sea to the east of the isles where the seals had their homes was one less ill-favored by nature. It was, perhaps, half a day's journey away by sail with a fair wind blowing. One of the larger of the man-isles, it had upon it not only two towns and a handful of scattered farms, but a castle, and in that castle lived the young Lord of the Isles.

He, like the Ron King, was big and powerful in build, and handsome as a picture. He had the look to him of a man who would brook no interference with his ideas or plans. Every lass who ever knew him would shiver with delight at the proud way of him, and sigh at the beauty of him, but he put his mind upon none of them, for in all his young years he had never yet seen the maid he felt he'd like to wed. So he held his head high and passed the lot of them by without more than half-seeing them. Still, it troubled him a bit, for he knew he'd reached the age when he should marry for the sake of the family.

He'd almost made up his mind to drop all the names of the lasses he least minded marrying into a creel and pick one out, and then get on with the wedding willy-nilly.

With that on his mind he went down to the quay, and got into his boat and set out for a sail. What with thinking over all the lasses he knew, and separating the possibles from the impossibles, maybe he wasn't paying too much attention to the way he was going. At any rate, what brought him up short was a voice calling almost in his ear, and sitting up there on the rock above him, and looking down at him, was a bit of a lassie.

"Man!" said she, "if you do not turn your boat she will break on the rocks."

The heart of the young Lord of the Isles turned three times upside-down in his breast, while he was turning his boat once away from the rocks. The boat he turned, but his head he didn't turn the same way, for he never took his eyes from her face.

"Bide there till I come!" he called to her, and then he put his eyes to the sea to find a place where he could come in to the isle. Three times around it he sailed, and the third time

83

he saw a narrow stretch of clear water where he might hope no sharp rocks lay in wait for the boat below the water, and win or lose in he went and brought the boat up safe on a narrow spit of sand. He leaped from his boat, and up the rocks he climbed, and there at the top was the lass.

"Who are you?" he demanded, "and how did you come here?"

"I am the daughter of the King Ron," said she, "and I live here."

He didn't know did he believe her or did he not! It might be true or she might be daft, but what he said next he had to say.

"Will you marry me?" said he.

"That I cannot say," said she, "till my father comes back and tells me."

"And when will he come back then?" asked the young Lord of the Isles.

"Who can say?" she answered. "Perhaps tomorrow. Perhaps even today. But I think it will more likely be a week away."

"I'll be back in a week at this same hour and ask him myself," said he. And he turned and went back down to his boat, and sailed home to his own isle and to his great gray castle.

A week to the hour and he was back again, and she was there on the rock waiting for him.

"Has your father returned?" he asked her.

"Not yet," said she, but her eyes were on the sea. She lifted her arm and pointed. "He is coming now," she said.

All he saw was a silver streak far out on the western sea. Nearer and nearer it came, and then the young lord saw for a minute the shining shape of a great sleek seal. It flashed close by, and disappeared behind the rocky cliff of the isle.

Then up from the rocks came the King of the Ron, by

inches broader and by inches taller than the young lord himself. A giant of a man was the King Ron, with a frown like a thundercloud on his brow and a flash of anger like lightning in his eyes and thunder itself from his mouth.

"And who are you, who dares to trespass upon the lands of the Ron!" he roared. A fearsome sight he was to see, in his wrath.

But the young lord came from a race that bred no cowards. He stood his ground and he faced the Ron and he answered firm and clear. "The Lord of the Isles am I!" said he, "and I have come to ask your leave to wed your daughter."

The Ron was struck to silence, and for a while he stood frowning at the Lord of the Isles. Then the thunder cleared from his brow and the lightning from his eyes, and he turned to his daughter. "Fearcharagh, Fearcharagh," he said tenderly, "what have you to say to that?"

The lass said nothing at all, but her eyes begged for what she would not put into words.

The Ron sighed a great deep sigh, and then he said sadly, "What there is to be said has already been said, for I see you are both of the same mind."

The three stood facing each other, and there was no sound at all but the wind blowing in the dry grass and the waves clawing at the rocks and the gulls shrieking high overhead.

Then the Ron Mor said at last, "Come back in a month, Man, if you are of the same mind then. And if you come back bring with you such garments as the women among you wear, for my daughter may take nothing with her when she leaves the Kingdom of the Ron."

"With nothing I will take her," said the young Lord of the Isles proudly. "She needs no other dower than herself when she becomes my bride!"

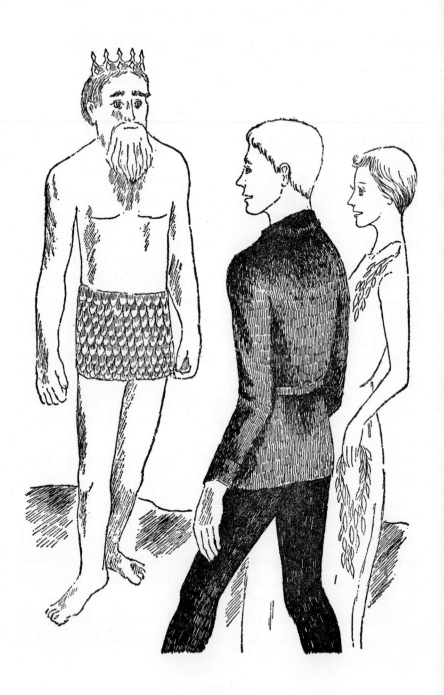

Then the young lord took her by the hand and looked deep into her eyes. "I will return," said he.

When the month had passed the Lord of the Isles came back as he had promised. He brought with him undergarments of fine linen and lace, as soft and white as the froth that tipped the sea waves. He brought a gown of rarest silk woven to his own order, that shimmered with green and blue and gold, like the sea with the sun upon it. He brought a golden coronet, jeweled with sea pearls, to set upon Fionna's soft golden brown hair, which she wore cut short upon her neck in the fashion of the seal-women.

When she had dressed herself in the garments she was the loveliest thing to see that had ever met the Lord of the Isles' eyes. Only she went barefooted, for the young lord had forgotten to bring her any shoes to wear.

When she was ready the Ron said heavily, "Guard her well, Man, for you have taken the brightest jewel in the crown of the King of the Ron." Then he took the young lord's hand in his left hand and his daughter's hand in his right. To his daughter he spoke and he said to her, "This you must promise! If ever an unkind word should pass the lips of your husband when he speaks to you, you must return to the Kingdom of the Ron!"

"I do so promise!" said she.

"This must you, too, promise! If ever an unkind word should pass your lips and you should speak to her in anger she must leave you without hindrance and return to the Kingdom of the Ron."

The Lord of the Isles laughed loud and the Lord of the Isles laughed long, in scorn at the thought of unkindness between himself and Fionna.

"I do so promise!" he said readily.

"And this, too," said the Ron. "With nothing she goes from me. Returning, she must bring nothing with her."

"Yes!" said they.

Then the King of the Ron joined their hands together, and he turned and went down over the rocks away from them.

They went down to the young lord's boat and got in, and sailed away to the island where his castle was. But the Ron did not see them leave, for there was no more to be seen of him by then but a silver streak on the far-off sea, going always to the northward.

The young lord and his bride came in to his island, and there at the quay was a great shining coach with four white horses waiting to carry them up to the castle. All the people of town and countryside were lined along the way to welcome them home. And because she was very young and very beautiful they loved her at sight. They wondered where the young lord had found her, but when they saw her feet without shoes they thought she was a country lass that the Lord of the Isles had found in his travels on the mainland. So they called her "the barefoot bride," but they thought no less of her because of that. When they got to know her better their love knew no bounds, for she was ever kind and gentle in all her ways with them.

So a year and a year and two more years went by, and the young lord and his wife were happy in their castle by the sea. At the end of the third year a baby lay in the cradle, and the young lord had his son and heir. It seemed then that no cloud could ever dim their happiness.

But a young wife is tied by the heartstrings to her child and cannot always rise and leave at her lord's bidding. It often happened that the Lord of the Isles would wish to go here and there, but the young wife would say that she must stay at home.

Proud as he was of his son this did not always suit the young lord's fancy, for in the first years where he wished to go, there she went too, and many a high junketing time they had together where all was new and wonderful to her and he the lad to show it all to her.

Now, too often, when he asked her to come with him, she would shake her head and say that the child needed her. "Have patience," she would say with a smile. "Soon he will be older and I will come with you then."

Then the Lord of the Isles would go off alone, and that did not please him at all. But although he did not complain to Fionna, patience was what he did not have at all, so it happened that soon he was away from the castle more than he was in it.

It was one of these times that the Lord of the Isles came back, and found his wife sitting at the window looking out over the sea. He had left her overlong, this time, for he had gone so far as the mainland with a party of friends and they had been delayed there over the night. He thought she looked lonely, and his conscience hurt him that he had left her so long, and he was angry with himself for his carelessness toward her. He was much too proud to say so and he shut it in.

The baby lying in his cradle was roaring away in grand style, and his mother paying no attention to it, knowing, as mothers do, that there are times when nothing ails them at all, but babies must cry in order to grow.

But the racket gave the Lord of the Isles a handle for his wrath, to turn it against somebody else, since pride would not let him turn it to himself. "In the name of heaven, Fionna," he cried angrily, "is there not some way you can keep the wee lad quiet!"

She turned herself upon the window seat and slowly she rose to her feet, with her great dark eyes fixed sadly upon his face.

"Oh my lord, my lord," she said reproachfully. She went to the cradle where the babe now lay quiet, having finished his crying for the time. She picked up the child and kissed him, once on each cheek and once on his brow and once on his small rosy mouth, and laid him back gently in his cradle again. Then she went out of the room.

The Lord of the Isles sat down in the window seat, and waited for his love to come back again. He waited long, and the baby slept, but still she did not return. So he went in search of her, through every room in the castle. From room to room he hunted, but she was in none of them. The cook and the scullery maids had seen no hair of her, and the gardener had not seen her since the morn. Her horse stood idle in its stall in the stables, and the grooms had not seen her all the day.

So he sat down on a stone bench by the gate lodge to wait again, thinking she'd gone to the village and thinking, too, that it was strange she had not told him she was going, as she always had before.

And then he remembered the promise they had made to the Ron!

Down to the sea he tore, with his heart racing faster than his feet. But he was too late.

There on the rocks lay her clothes, piled in a tidy heap, and far out on the sea a silver streak moved swiftly away from him.

And so Fionna Nic Mor Ailean returned to the Kingdom of the Ron, according to the promise she had made to her father.

For the Lord of the Isles had spoken to her in anger, and there was nothing else that she could do. And as she had brought nothing with her, so too, by the terms of her promise, she took nothing back with her. For she left her babe in his cradle, her lord in his castle, and her clothes on the rocky shore.

The Lord of the Isles went back into his castle, and shut himself up in his room. For a long week he had no word with anyone, and if he ate a bite or drank a sup no one knew of it. But when, on the seventh day, he came out, it was as if he were a different man. He, who had been wayward and proud, was gentle and humble. He, who had ruled with arrogance, was just and kind. No one in all the years to come ever heard an unkind word from him. And never did he allow Fionna's name to be mentioned to him, though all who knew her grieved that she was gone and would have sorrowed with him had he allowed it.

So it went until his child and Fionna's had grown to be a man. On the day the lad reached his twenty-first year there was a great celebration because of it, and people came from the mainland and from all the towns of the islands. Before the banquet was over, while all were gathered together, the lord handed the keys to the castle and a deed to all he possessed to his son. The lad would have refused the gift, but his father pressed it on him, so the son laid the papers and keys aside and thought to take the matter up with his father upon the next day.

But while all were feasting, the Lord of the Isles rose from the table and went down to the quay, and getting into his boat set sail to the westward. And he never came back again.

Where did he go? Well, there were many stories about that. Some said that he sailed far out on the great western ocean and was lost there in the high green waves. Some said that

he sailed until he reached Tir-nan-Og, the Isles of the Blest, to live forever there in happiness with the saints he had grown to resemble.

But the fishermen, who tell the tale, say that he simply sailed to the island of the King of the Ron, taking nothing with him but himself, for his boat with all his clothes in it was found days later halfway between the quay of his own island and the mainland, right side up and with no harm done to it.

And the fishermen say that he stayed at the castle to do his duty by his son until he became a man and could go on by himself, for his father could not take him with him, any more than Fionna could when she returned to her father.

And they say that the King of the Ron took him in, for the sake of the love he and Fionna still had for each other, and gave him the power of the Ron Mor to change himself from man to seal at will.

In proof of this the fishermen say that where they once saw one great man in the mists of the dawning day on the rocks of the seals, they now see two, and with them often, a woman who sits and sings more wildly and sweetly than ever before.

So the end of the tale is a happy one, with Fionna and the Lord of the Isles together in the Kingdom of the Ron, after all the long unhappy years.

Their son lived on in the great gray castle, and became the new Lord of the Isles in his father's stead. A good one he was, too, for he followed the rule of his father, whose motto was "be kind."

Spin, Weave, Wear

THERE WAS A LASS of Kintiemuir once, and she was a grand hand at spinning and weaving and sewing, and she was awful bonnie besides.

She was the only daughter of a well-off farmer, and as there was only herself and her father at home she looked after him and kept his house and kept her eye on the maids in the dairy.

He was so proud of her and she was so dear to him that he wouldn't have any other father's child praised above her. And as he was a great one for talking, sometimes he let his tongue run away with him and say more than he meant.

One day he went over to another town to see about some cattle he heard was going for sale there. And after the sales were over he sat down to dinner at the inn with a lot of other farmers who had come to town for the sales.

The dinner was a good one, and most of the farmers were pleased with the deals they'd made, so they didn't hurry home, but sat there, talking, at the table.

Well they talked about one thing then another, and at last they began to talk about their lads and lasses at home. Not boasting they weren't, to be sure, but each giving his own lad or lass their due.

One farmer said his lass, maybe, wasn't the bonniest ever seen, though she was bonny enough to have her choice of the lads. But she was not likely to find her match when it came to baking and cooking, and the laird's cook herself had agreed to that.

Another farmer's lad was maybe a little too scrawny and undersized ever to make much of a farmer, but, losh, he was the lad for learning. Always his nose in a book, he had. He knew more now than the Dominie himself, so his mother and himself had decided they'd make him into a minister.

And so it went, with one father's lass doing one thing and another's lad doing another, all better than anyone ever had heard of anywhere!

The farmer of Kintiemuir sat there listening, and the more he listened, the madder he got inside, to think any of them would try to claim a bairn who could do better than his own lass at home!

So when it came to his turn he said, easy and quiet-like, as if it didn't matter much, "Och, my lass is none so bad. She's awful bonny, to be sure, but that doesn't count at all, against what she can do. For she can spin in the morning, and weave in the afternoon, and sew in the evening, and when you rise from your bed in the morn your new clothes is all laid out ready for you to wear!"

All the farmers gawped at him, for they'd ne'er heard the like! And when they went away after dinner all they could talk about was the wonderful ways of the lass of Kintiemuir.

The farmer went home and told his daughter what he'd said.

"Och now," said she, "you ne'er should have said that, for you know there's no truth in it!" But she smiled at him lovingly, because she knew it was his pride and his love that made him tell such a terrible big fib. And then she put it out of her mind, not being the sort to fret over what was too late to mend.

But that sort of news travels faster by word of mouth than ever the king's messengers could carry it. In no time at all everybody the length and breadth of Scotland had heard of the lass, and the tales lost naught in the telling!

At last it reached the ear of the king in his great castle, and as things were dull in the place at the time he sent for the lass to come there and try her skill against any of the lasses in the land who thought they might do as well as she could.

When the summons came that she was to come to the court for the match by the end of the second fortnight to come, the lass couldn't think what she was ever going to do about it all!

Being one for thinking and not for weeping she sat down by the fire to see what she could do about it. Her father was about, somewhere on the farm with the men, but there was no need to worrit him about it.

To the court she must go, since the king himself had sent for her. But what was she going to do when she got there? She knew, as sure as black is black and white is white, that she could not spin thread and weave cloth and sew garments all in one day. The only other way out would be to tell the king the truth—that her father had told a lie because he loved her so much and was so proud of her. Of course, she couldn't shame her father so, and besides the king might be angry and throw the poor dearie into prison for telling such a fib.

As she sat there by the fire by herself, "Och, father," she sighed, "you meant no harm, but just see the pickle you've got us in!"

She couldn't shame her father, and she couldn't do what he

said she could, and if there was a third way out she didn't know what it was.

"There's no way out at all," said she, mournfully.

"Happen there is!" said her big black cat, who sat watching her from t'other side of the hearth.

The lass jumped, and she stared at her cat. "Is it yourself that's talking, Tom?" she asked, not believing her ears.

"Och aye," said the cat, and he added carelessly, "I can do so, if there's aught I'm caring to say. And anyone I'm caring to say it to."

"Oh," said the lass.

"Well," said the cat, "this is a time for talking."

"There's naught to say," said the lass. "I've mulled it o'er and o'er and I cannot do it."

"Well then," said the cat wisely, "you must be helped."

The lass looked at the cat and smiled. "How could you help me, Tom?" she asked.

"Not me," said the cat hastily, "but there might be ways."

"How?" asked she.

"You would not like to become a witch, I doubt?" asked the cat slyly.

"I would not!" said the lass.

"Och aye. I thought not," said the cat with a great sigh. "Then we'll have to see if we can get one to help us. 'Twould be easier," he coaxed, "to turn you into a witch and let you manage for yourself."

"No!" said the lass.

"Well," said the cat, resigned-like, "every self-respecting cat has a friend or two among the witches. Open the door for me, mistress, and I'll go see what I can do."

She opened the door and out he leapt and in a minute was gone.

He never came back till a night and a day and another night had passed. Then in the morning early, when the lass was stirring the porridge on the back of the fire, he scratched at the door. He stalked in, with his tail lashing proudly from side to side. His fur was tangled and torn, but he had a satisfied look on his face and he grinned at her through his whiskers.

"Well?" said she.

" 'Tis done!" said he. "And tonight is the night to settle it!"

So that night he led the lassie out on the moor. They went a long way till they came to a deep dark glen, and into the glen the black cat went and the lassie followed after.

When they came to the end of the glen they saw a wee bit fire in the cleft ahead of them. And when they got up close they saw two old crones crouched over the fire, one on either side of it.

The cat went up boldly and greeted them. "This is the lassie I was telling you about," said he.

They peered at her through the smoke of the fire, but said naught.

"So then," said the cat, "let us get to the bargain. What will you take to lay the spell we need?"

The two witches laid their heads together and whispered to each other for a while. Then they asked, "Is it a spell for a day or a week or a month or a year you're wanting?"

"A day or a week or a month might not be long enough," said the lass. "And a year might be too long. Can you not make it to last till I no longer need it?"

The two crones whispered together again, and then one of them said, "Aye. But it would be harder and come higher. And there would be a condition to it."

"What will ye take for the spell?" growled the cat, who was growing impatient.

"Two new brooms that have ne'er touched ground," said the first old witch.

"Aye," said the lass, for she could bind brooms as well as she could weave.

"Two flasks of water that the sun has never shone upon," said the second witch.

"Aye," said the lass, for she knew where she'd be getting that, too.

"Two bits of silver out of a Gypsy lad's pocket," said the first witch again.

"Aye," said the cat, for that he could take care of himself.

"Two rings of gold that was never mined or minted."

At that the lass looked at the cat, and the cat looked at the lass, for she did not know where that could be found, nor did he, as she well knew. But before she could up and say so, the cat said, "Aye!"

So the bargain was made, and the two witches told them to come back the next night with the things they'd promised, and then they'd get on with the spell.

On the way home the cat said, "You get the brooms and the water on the morrow, and I'll get the silver pieces ere I come home tonight."

"But who will get the two golden rings?" cried the lassie.

"Not I!" said the cat airily. "You can be putting your mind to that!" And with a flip of his tail off he went, and vanished into the darkness.

When the cat got to the place where the Gypsies had their camp he went about until he found a likely looking lad, sleeping on a heap of rags away from the rest of the Gypsies.

The cat got busy and worked very gently until he'd chewed a hole in the Gypsy lad's pocket. So slyly did the cat work, that although the Gypsy stirred once or twice he never woke

up at all. When the hole was big enough the cat gave the lad a scratch with one of his claws. The Gypsy lad jumped up to his feet to find out what had bitten him, and all his money fell out through the hole in his pocket. While he was hunting around picking it up the cat grabbed two silver pieces in his mouth and ran off with them, and the Gypsy lad none the wiser!

The next morning the lass came down early and there was the cat on the doorstep. He came into the room and jumped up on the table and there he laid down the two bits of silver he had been holding in his mouth.

"There!" said he with a yawn. "I've been out all the night and I'm tired out, so I'm going to sleep." He curled up in a corner near the fire and stirred no more that day.

When her father came down the lass gave him his porridge, and after he had gone out to his fields she took a hatchet and a sharp knife in her apron pocket and off she went to the forest. She hunted about until she found two straight young trees that were about the size round of a broomstick. She cut them off well above the ground with her hatchet, and then she tied them on her back so that they couldn't touch the ground.

Next she climbed high up into a beech tree, and cut a big bundle of thin twigs with her knife, and those she tied upon her back, too. Then she went home.

When she got there she peeled the sticks and trimmed the twigs and made the brooms, binding them with new woolen yarn. From the first to the last nothing about them ever touched ground, so that much was as it should be. Next she took two stone flasks to fetch the water in. She knew where to get that, for behind the scullery there was a shed and under the floor of the shed was a well. There were no windows in the shed and the well was covered with a great flat stone, so the sun never came anywhere near the water. The lass filled the flasks and put the stoppers in, and then she took them back into the house. She laid the brooms and the silver and the flasks of water on a shelf, and now all she had to be finding was the two rings of gold—and where she'd be getting them, she did not know at all!

She sat down on a stool by the hearth to think about it, and whilst she was sitting she took down her hair and began to comb it, to tidy it. As she was combing it a hair fell from her comb and lay upon her knee. She looked at it, shining in the firelight, and thought how it looked like gold.

Then she laughed aloud. For it was gold, unmined and unminted, and just what the old witchwomen had asked for!

So she cut a few strands from her head and plaited them into rings, and bound them and wound them until they were smooth and round. Then she laid them on the shelf with the brooms and the flasks of water and the silver pieces. Now she had all that she needed.

Her father came in and she gave him his supper, and then he went to bed. When he was asleep the lass woke up the cat. She put the silver pieces and the gold rings in her pocket and tied the brooms on her back. She took a flask under each arm, and set off with the black cat to the witches' glen.

When she got there she gave the witches all she had brought. And now would they give her the magic spell?

"Not so fast!" they told her. "Time and other things are needed to make a spell that will hold good. You'll have to fetch us what we cannot get for ourselves, since we are not able to leave this place at present."

The black cat grumbled very loud when he heard that, but there was no help for it. They said that they could not make

103

the spell without these things, and since they could not go and get them the lass and the cat would have to be fetching them.

"What are they then?" growled the cat.

"Three sacks of thistledown, gathered from three fields in the dark of the moon," said the first witch.

"Three sacks of wheat straw from the parson's byre," said the second witch.

"Three long black thorns pulled from the bush at the kirk door at the stroke of midnight," said both of the witches together.

The next night there was no moon, so the black cat and the lass went back and forth through the fields gathering thistledown. And a terrible hard task it was in the darkness.

The night after that they went to the parson's byre and filled three sacks full of wheat straw.

The third night they went to the kirk, and right on the toll of midnight they pulled three long black thorns from the bush at the door.

Then they went back to the glen.

The witches took the thistledown and passed it through the smoke of the fire, one sackful at a time. And what they sang as they passed it through no one can ever tell, for they sang in a language only witches know. When they had finished, they gave the sacks back to the lass. Two of the sacks were filled with what looked like the finest carded wool, but the third sack had flax tow in it.

"Use these for your spinning," the witches said. "You will spin three lots of thread, one by one, and when you put the wool on the distaff the wheel will turn of itself, and faster than mortal hand could ever turn it, and if you leave it then to itself by the morning's end your spinning will all be done."

Then they seized the wheat straw and threw it into a tub. They leached it and heckled it and wrung it out and combed it. Then they passed it back and forth through the smoke, while they sang their witches' song. And when they were through they had three hanks of yarn. Two were like soft, soft wool, but the other one was like fine white linen. They gave these to the lass, too.

"You will weave three webs of cloth," they told her. "After you've had your dinner use these to set the warp, one by one. As soon as you thread the shuttle the loom will start to weave by itself, faster than mortal hand could ever throw the shuttle. Leave it alone, except to set the warp and thread the shuttle each time, and by the end of the afternoon your weaving will all be done."

Then they passed the black thorns through the smoke in the same way, and when they were done, they handed the lass three shining needles.

"After you've had your supper," said they, "cut out your cloth and thread your needles, and set one in each garment as it lays cut for the sewing. As soon as you set the needles to the cloth they will start to stitch, faster than mortal hand could ever sew, and by the time that midnight strikes, the garments will all be done."

The lass started to thank them, but they stopped her.

"We told you a condition came with the spell," they said, "and here it is. From the time you step over the threshold of the king's castle until you return to your father's house you must not speak one word. If you do, the magic spell will be broken, and you will no longer have the power we have given you."

Aye, the lass understood, and not a word would pass her lips. She would be sure to mind that well.

Then each of the witches slipped one of the golden rings on a finger and hung one of the stone flasks by its handle on one of the broomsticks. "Now we can leave this place!" said they, and they each mounted a broom, and striking the broomstick with a silver piece they cried, "Off and away!" Up they flew into the sky and soon were out of sight.

So the lass and the black cat went home, taking the witches' wares along with them.

On the day appointed the lass came to the king's castle with her father.

She had told her father nothing at all about the help she had got from the witches. All she had said was that she had it in her mind not to say a word while she was at the king's court, so he could just be doing the talking for both of them. That suited him fine, for he was overfond of talking, which will be understood, since it was his tongue that had caused all her trouble.

In all the country there had been found only three lasses who were willing to try to match the lass of Kintiemuir, although the king's heralds had gone up and down through the land proclaiming the contest, and the king had offered a prize of gold to the one who came out ahead. All the others got discouraged before they could begin when they heard what was said about the farmer's daughter.

Since the three other lassies had not yet come, the lassie and her father had to wait till they got there. There was a great crowd of lords, and ladies, and gentlemen come to see who would win, and they all liked the lassie well.

But though she would smile or nod or shake her head, not one word would she say. As for her father, he talked enough for a half a dozen, and would have made his story about her even bigger had she not kept beside him all the time with her hand on his arm to stop him when his tales flew too high. You see, he'd told it so often he'd begun to believe it himself!

Among the gentleman was one young laird who had decided the minute she stepped in at the door that she was the one he wanted to wed. So he followed her wherever she went, and as she would not talk to him, he talked to her. Since he never could find her away from her father, the second day he asked her to marry him, in spite of the father being there. The father was willing enough, but it seemed the lass wasn't, for she only smiled and shook her head and led the old man away to the other end of the castle.

The young laird sulked for a day or two, and then the other lassies came, and the next day they were going to begin the match.

The young laird caught her as she was going up the stairs that night and again he asked her to wed him, but again she smiled and shook her head and went away up the stairs to her bed.

So he almost decided to ride away, but then he didn't after all, for he wasn't the kind to give up so easy when he wanted her so bad.

The next morning the king's servants woke all the lassies up early, and they took each one to a separate room, high up under the roof of the castle. There was naught in each room but a spinning wheel, a loom, a table, and a chair. On the table in the room was a heap of wool and tow, and a pair of shears and a needle. Besides that there was only a tray which held the food for the day.

When the servant had gone away and left her and shut the door behind him the lass started in. She paid no attention to what was on the table for she had brought her own things with her.

She set the wool from the first bag on the distaff and at once the wheel began to turn so fast she could hardly see it. When it stopped, she took off the big ball of thread that was there and started it again. Three times she set it that morning, and when the big bell in the courtyard rang at noon she was through with the spinning and the sacks were all empty, but she had three balls of thread.

Then she took the cover off the tray and sat down at the table and ate a good dinner, making sure to leave enough of the food for suppertime.

Then she covered up the tray again and brushed up the crumbs and put them out of the window for the birds.

Now she was through with her dinner, so she took the first ball of the witches' warp and set the loom. Then she threaded the shuttle with thread from the first ball that had been spun in the morning. The minute she threaded the shuttle it jerked itself out of her hand, and the loom began to weave all by itself. Click-clack! Clack-clickety-clack! Clickety-clickey-clickety-clack! Faster and faster and faster, till her eye couldn't see the shuttle as it flew back and forth.

But as it wove the cloth took color, where before all had been white. Three times she set the warp and threaded the shuttle that afternoon, and when the bell in the courtyard tolled for eventide she had three big webs of cloth. One was of fine dark green wool and one was the king's own plaid, but the third one was linen so fine it felt like the richest silk.

So then she sat down to her supper and ate with a good appetite. When she had finished, she piled up the dishes on the tray and laid the cover on it again, and set the tray in the hall. Then she brushed up the crumbs and threw them out of the window.

Then she was ready to get on with the work. She lit a candle to see by, for it was getting dark. Then she took up her shears and began to cut her cloth. She cut a jacket and trews from the green cloth, and a kilt from the plaid, and from the fine white linen she cut a shirt.

When she had finished with the cutting she took the witches' needles from her pocket and threaded them with some of the thread that was left over. She set a needle into each of the garments, and at once they began to stitch away, all by themselves and so fast she couldn't even see them. And when the bell in the courtyard tolled for midnight there lay upon the table a fine green coat and a pair of trews, a fine plaid kilt, and a white ruffled shirt, all so well made that the king himself could not scorn them.

The lassie took up the garments and blew out the candle, and went down to bed. She was that tired out with watching things work that she fell asleep in the middle of a yawn, and never woke till the sun was high in the morning.

She got up and dressed herself, then she rang for a servant and showed him by signs that he was to take the garments to the king. After that she went down to her breakfast.

There was nobody in the great dining hall when she got there, for the king was so delighted with the garments he had put them on at once and sent for all the court to come and see. So everyone was up with the king saying, "Oh!" and "Ah!" and "Och well now!"

But while the lassie was eating her porridge in came the young laird, and him in a terrible taking. He came right up to her where she sat at the big long table all by herself.

And he said to her, said he, "I've asked you once and I've asked you twice and I'll ask you again, and then I'll ask no more. For if you won't wed me, I'll go away and look for some-body else! Will you have me?"

She swallowed the porridge she had in her mouth and she answered quick, "I'll have you!" Then she dropped her spoon in her porridge bowl and cried out, "Lawks! I've destroyed the magic spell!"

Well, then she had to tell him the whole story, but when he heard it he said he didn't mind at all. He wouldn't want his wife spinning and weaving and sewing, and besides he always got his clothes from the tailor. When she saw he didn't mind then she didn't either, for the spell had lasted as long as she needed it, which was what the witches had promised.

And what about the other lassies? Well, the first one was half done, the second one was a third done, and the third one hadn't started at all, for when she saw the big heap of wool she got so discouraged that she just sat down and cried all day.

But the king was a good-natured, pleasant king, so he gave each of the three lassies a kind word and thanked them for coming, and sent them away with a fine present, and happy anyway.

Everybody agreed that the lass of Kintiemuir had fairly won the prize. The king was so pleased that he doubled the prize, which made a grand dower for the lassie to bring to her lord.

The king took such pleasure from his new clothes that the lass and her laird never told him it was all done by magic. There was nobody else could tell him, for nobody else knew but the witches and the lassie's big black cat. The witches were gone for good, and as for the big black cat—he'd stopped talking!

So the king gave the two of them a grand wedding, and all the lords and ladies and gentlemen came and danced merrily at it. After they were married, the lassie's father sold his farm and stayed at the court, for the king liked to hear him talk.

But the lassie and the laird and the big black cat rode off to the laird's castle and they all lived there happily ever after.

The Bogles from the Howff

There was once a young doctor of learning who was sore troubled with bogles. He was the only son of an old couple to whom he had been born when they were getting along in years, and as they were determined to make a man of learning of him and had the brass to pay for it he had been little at home since he was a bit of a lad, being off and away at one school or another most of his days. He went to day school, and to grammar school, then to a Scottish public school. Then he went to the University of Edinboro', and after that to various universities here and there about the face of Europe. While he was away getting all this schooling his mother and father got older and older, and at last they got so old they died of it, both satisfied that they'd done their best for their son.

By that time he'd got all the knowledge he thought he needed, and he decided it was time to come home to the house his parents had left him and write a book about all the things he'd learned.

So back he came and settled into the house.

He found that it was a dreary old house in a dreary old

113

street in the heart of the old part of Dundee, where the smoke from all the chimneys of the town had hung over it for long, long years. The Dundee Law seemed to tower over it and want to shut it in, although it was really not so near as it looked. But the house stood close by the Howff, that ancient graveyard which has held the honored and famous dead of the town for over three hundred years.

The house was as dark and dismal inside as it was without. The walls were dark and damp and of no sort of color you could lay a name to. There were great wooden blinds to the windows that kept the light out, for his mother had always said the light would fade the carpet.

Why he should stay there in the dank old place at an age when other young men were out enjoying themselves was a queer sort of riddle. Maybe he couldn't have told the answer to it himself, if he'd ever thought about it at all.

There was no lack of money, for he'd been left plenty. But he was a quiet, steady young man and his wants were few, and maybe he was just glad to settle down in peace after all the traveling around from one school to another. So he took the house the way it was and let it be.

His father and mother had never told him about the bogles, and maybe they never noticed them at all, but he soon found out about them for himself.

When he settled in he looked about till he found himself a cook and a lass to keep house for him. The two of them came with their boxes and took over. But after they'd been there a day or two the cook came to him and said, "There's somewhat amiss with the garret, maister."

"What would it be?" he asked.

"The draughts is terrible," she told him. "Ye canna keep a door ajar, but a breeze comes by and bangs it shut. And the locks won't hold, for as soon as it's shut, the draught bangs it wide open again. What with banging and creaking all the night the lass and me can get no sleep at all!"

"Well, move down to the next storey," said the doctor. "I'll have in a man to look to the garret."

The man came and looked to the garret, but he could find naught wrong, for the windows were tight and he couldn't find the sign of a place for the draught to come in.

But a few days later the doctor came down to his breakfast to find the boxes of the two women in the hall and the women beside them, white as winding sheets.

The cook spoke for both of them. "We'll be leaving ye, maister," said she, "this very morning's morn!"

"Why then?" asked the astonished doctor.

"We'll not be staying in a place where there's bogles!" said the cook firmly. The serving lass shrieked a wee shriek and rolled her eyes and clutched the cook's arm.

"Bogles!" The doctor laughed. "You mean ghosts? Oh come, come now! You are a sensible woman. You know there are no such things as ghosts!"

"I know what I know!" said the cook.

Then the two of them picked up their boxes and out of the door they went, without waiting to ask could they get their wages!

Well that was the way it was after that. The doctor would find himself a new couple of women to look after the house. They'd come with their boxes and all, but after a few days the boxes were down in the hall and the women beside them ready to go their ways, and all because of the bogles!

Two by two they came, and two by two they went, over and over again, and not even the promise of better wages would tempt them to stay.

115

And at last came a time when the doctor could find no one who would come at all, for the ones who left had spread the news wide and there wasn't a lass in the town of Dundee who'd step a foot into the doctor's house. No! Not even for all the money in Dundee!

Then the doctor took the ferry over the Tay to Newport, thinking maybe he could find a cook and housemaid there. But the news of the doctor's bogles had got to Newport before him, being the sort of news that travels fast. The Newport lassies who were willing to go into service would have nothing at all to do with him, after they found out who he was.

It came into his mind then that he'd heard that they had a wheen of ghosts in St. Andrews. Maybe the women there'd be used to them, and wouldn't be minding a house that was said to have bogles in it.

Not that he believed in bogles himself. No indeed. Not he!

So he made the journey from Newport to St. Andrews. But he had no luck there at all. There were bogles galore, 'tis true. In fact the place must have been teeming with them, for the folks at St. Andrews told him proudly that there was scarcely a house in the town that hadn't a bogle or two in it—certainly not one of the older houses.

But the trouble with St. Andrews was that if there were no lack of bogles, there were no lassies who weren't already in service. And they all said they were suited fine where they were, thank you, and wouldn't like to be making a change, even for the bigger wages the doctor was willing to pay.

So it looked as if he'd just have to do for himself, though he didn't know how to cook at all, and as for cleaning up and making things tidy he knew less about that.

He started back home again, for there was nothing else he could do.

When he was on the ferry going back from Newport to Dundee he saw a lass on the boat. She was the sort of a lass you look twice at, for she had the reddest hair in the world, springing up in wee curls in the fresh wind from the Tay. She had the white skin that goes with that sort of hair, and a saucy nose with a sprinkle of freckles across it, and eyes of the bluest blue he'd ever seen.

She was neat as a silver pin, too, with a little flat straw hat pinned tight to her curls and a white blouse and a tidy black skirt. But what he noticed most was her smile, for it was merry and kind.

He thought she wouldn't be minding if he went and spoke to her. So he went over and stood beside her at the rail of the boat.

"Do you believe in bogles?" he asked her.

She looked at him and her eyes crinkled, and she broke into a laugh. "Och do I not!" she cried. "My old grannie at Blairgowrie that I'm going to stay with had a rare time with a pair of them a year or so back, till she rid them out!"

"Oh," said he.

"Do you not believe in them?" asked the red-haired lass curiously.

"No I don't!" said he.

And that was the end of that, for if she believed in bogles there was no use asking her to come and keep house for him, because she would not stay any more than the rest of them.

When he got back home he went into the scullery to see what there was for his supper. But what was there that had to be cooked, he didn't know what to do with. He just had to make do with the heel of a loaf of bread and a bit of stale cheese that wasn't fit to bait a mousetrap with.

117

So when he went into his study he was hungry and he was tired and he was plain put about!

He sat down at his desk, and he banged his fist on it, and he shouted out loud! "'Tis all nonsense! THERE ARE NO BOGLES!"

"Oh, aren't there?" asked a quiet voice behind him.

He whirled around in his chair, and then his eyes bugged out and his hair stood straight up on his head.

There were three big white things standing there, *and he could see right through them.*

But the doctor was awful stubborn. "There are no bogles," he said again, only his voice wasn't so loud this time and he didn't sound as if he was so sure about it.

"Then what would you be calling us?" asked one of them politely.

Well, there was no two ways about it. Bogles they were, and BOGLES he had to call them. So he had to admit that there *were* bogles in his house.

What he didn't know yet was how many of them were there. Because they liked his house fine. It was so nice and dark and damp.

It was not so bad as far as his meals went, for he was taking them at the inn, rather than starve at home. But at home he was fair distracted, for it seemed as if there were more and more bogles all the time.

Bogles peered down at him from over the rail of the staircase, and there were always some of them lurking about in the corners of any room he was in, blinking their eyes at him and sighing at him, and they fair gave him a chill. The three first ones followed him about, and when he went up to his bed at night they came along and sat on the foot of the bed and talked to him.

They all came from the Howff, they told him.

"Och aye," sighed one of them. " 'Twas a fine graveyard, one time."

"For the first hundred years or so," said the second bogle.

"But after that it began to get crowded. A lot of new people got brought in, and some of them wasn't the sort we'd want to neighbor with," said the first one again.

But since they had found his place they told the doctor, 'twas far better. They liked it fine in his house, and all the best bogles were moving over there, too, so they felt much more at home than they did in the Howff.

Things being the way they were the doctor had no peace by day or by night. He was writing away on his learned book about some sort of wisdom or other, I wouldn't know what. He was having a hard time of it, for the bogles were that curious that they hung about him and peered over his shoulder, and even took to criticizing what he wrote. One of them even got so familiar that he'd lean on the doctor's shoulder and point out places where the doctor could be doing better with his words. It annoyed the doctor a lot, because he found himself writing down what the bogle said, and he had ideas of his own that he liked better than the ones the bogle was giving him.

One day as he sat in the inn eating his dinner he made up his mind that he'd take no more of the bogles, for he had had enough!

So he went home and put on his best clothes for a journey, and off he went to Blairgowrie to find the red-haired lass and ask her what her grannie had done to rid herself of her bogles.

When he got to Blairgowrie he went about the town looking for the lass. He couldn't ask for her for he didn't know her name. By-and-by he got to the end of the town and there

he saw a neat little two-storey cottage, with a low stone wall around it, and inside of the wall a big garden full of flowers. There was a bench by the door of the cottage, and on the bench sat the red-haired lass, and she was still smiling.

"Good day!" says he.

"Good day!" says she. "I thought you'd soon be coming along."

"You did!" said he, surprised. "Why did you then?"

"Because you asked if I believed in bogles. So then I knew that you had some of your own and would be coming to find out what my grannie did to get rid of hers."

He was amazed that one so bonny could be so wise. So he opened the gate and went into the garden. He sat down on the bench beside her and told her all his trouble.

"Will you come and help me get them out of the house?" he asked, when he'd finished his story.

"Of course I will!" said she.

Then she took him in to her grannie. Her grannie was just like her, only her hair was white and she wasn't so young, but her eyes were just as blue and her smile was as merry and kind.

"Grannie," said the lass, "I'm going with this gentleman to keep house for him, and to rid him of some bogles he has at home."

"If anyone can, you can!" said her grannie, and the two of them laughed as if bogles were no trouble at all.

So the lass got ready and off she went with the doctor.

When he opened the door of his house and they went in, the lass wrinkled her nose and made a face. "Faugh!" said she. "It smells of bogle! A proper graveyard smell," she added, looking around at the place.

121

"They come from the Howff," he told her, as if that explained it.

"I'll be bound!" she said. "And to the Howff they'll go back!"

That night the doctor ate his meal at home, instead of going to the inn. It was a good one, too, for the lass got it, and nobody had ever said that she didn't know how to cook.

There wasn't a sign of a bogle that night, but that was because they were biding their time and looking the lass over.

The next morning the lass came into the study. She had on a blue overall, the same color as her eyes, and there was a fresh white kerchief tied to cover her hair.

"This is a proper dark old place," said she, looking about the room. "Why do you not throw back those big old blinds and open the windows to let a wee bit of sun and fresh air in?"

"My mother said it would let dust in and fade the carpets," the doctor said. He remembered that from the time when he was a wee lad, before he went off to his schools.

"What if it does!" said she. "Can you not buy new ones?"

"I never thought of that!" he said. "Of course I can."

So the lass pulled the curtains back and folded back the wooden blinds. Then she opened the windows wide and the sea air came pouring in from the harbor, with the sun riding on top of it.

"That's better!" the lass told him.

"It is, indeed!" said the doctor, as he took a long, deep breath of the fresh cool air.

But the red-haired lass took another look at the dingy old room and frowned. "No wonder you have bogles," she said. "I never saw a place they'd like better. But I can do no more for you till time for your dinner, so I'll leave you. I'm turning out the scullery."

122

So the doctor worked at his book and the lass worked at the scullery, and the day went by.

That night the bogles came in a crowd and gathered around the doctor's bed.

"Who is the red-haired lass in the house?" asked the first bogle.

"She's my new housekeeper," the doctor told them, yawning because he had worked awful hard on his learned book all day. The bogles hadn't come near him, because they didn't like all the sunlight that came into the study after the lass opened the windows.

"Is she going to stay here?" they asked.

"I hope so!" yawned the doctor. He had had a good supper, and he'd eaten a lot of it, and now he was so sleepy he couldn't keep his eyes open. Before the bogles had time to ask him anything else he'd fallen fast asleep.

They couldn't wake him for all they tried. So they gave him up and went to see could they scare the red-haired lass away, the same as they had the others. But she had worked hard and eaten well, too, so they couldn't waken her, no more than they could the doctor. They all agreed it was a bad day for the bogles when the lass came into the house. It was going to take an awful lot of hard work to get her out again.

The next day the red-haired lass was up early, and the day after that, and the next day after, too. The kitchen and the scullery were beginning to look like different places, for she swept and dusted and scrubbed and scoured and polished from morn to night. The doctor saw little of her except at mealtimes, but the meals were the best he'd ever had in his life, and she sat across the table from him and poured his tea and smiled at him.

At night he and the lass were so tired out, him with his

writing and her with her turning out, that they couldn't be bothered about the bogles.

The bogles were there, nonetheless. They'd brought a lot more bogles from the Howff to help them—even some of the riff-raff they'd moved to the doctor's house to get away from! There were plenty of dark old rooms in the house still, for the lass was still busy with the scullery and the kitchen and hadn't come off the ground floor yet.

So at night the bogles tried all their best tricks that never had failed before. They swept through the house like a tempest, banging doors open and shut, wailing and gibbering, moaning and mowing, clanking chains and rattling bones, and the like.

It all did no good. Nobody heard them except maybe a passer-by in the street, who thought it was the wind rising from the sea, and hurried home so as not to get caught in a storm.

When the end of the week came along the red-haired lass said to the doctor, "You'd best take your pens and paper and things over to my grannie's at Blairgowrie and do your writing there. I'm through with the kitchen and the scullery, and now I'm going to turn out the rest of the house."

He didn't want to go, but she told him he'd got to for he'd only be in her way.

"You can leave me some money to get some things I'll be needing, and to pay for help to come in, to do what I can't do myself," she told him. "And don't come back till I send for you, mind!"

So he packed up, and off he went to her grannie's house as she told him to.

As soon as he was gone, the red-haired lass started in again, and now she really showed what she could do. The bogles

124

were so upset about what was going on that one night they laid for her and caught her on the stairs as she was going up to her bed. They tried to look as grisly as they could, and the noises they made were something horrible.

But the red-haired lass only stared straight through them. "Go away you nasty things!" she said.

"We won't then!" they said indignantly. "We got here first and we've a mind to stay. Why don't you go away?"

"I like my work and I'm useful here," said the lass. "Which is more than you can say."

"It was all fine till you came," complained one of the bogles.

"It was all wrong till I came," said the lass right back at them. "And I wish you'd stop argy-bargying and let me get to my bed. I've a big day's work ahead of me tomorrow, for the painters are coming in and the men to take away the blinds, and when they're done 'twill be all sunny and bright and a treat to see!"

All the bogles groaned like one big groan.

"Sunny!" moaned one.

"Bright!" shrieked another.

"Well anyway, we're not going away," said they.

"Stay if you like," said the lass. "It's all one to me if you stay or go. But you won't like it!" she promised them. And with that she walked straight up the steps and through the lot of them, and went to bed and to sleep.

After that the battle between the bogles and the lass really began. You couldn't say they didn't put up a fight for it, but the lass was more than a match for them. She drove them from the first storey of the house to the second, and from the second to the third, and from the third to the garret, for they couldn't stand the sunlight and brightness that followed her as she went up through the house at her work.

126

At last they had to pack up their extra winding sheets and their chains and bones and things and go back to the graveyard they'd come from, for the house wasn't fit for a bogle to stay in, and even if the Howff was crowded it suited them better now.

Well, when the painters and carpenters and all were gone the lass found a serving maid to help her with the work. And this one stayed! But the lass didn't bother to look for a cook, for she thought her own cooking would suit the doctor best when he came back to his house.

The doctor was just as comfortable in her grannie's house and just as well fed there, and everything was fine, except that he missed the red-haired lass, for he'd begun to get used to having her around. There were no bogles to bother him at the lass's grannie's house, for she had rid herself of hers a long time ago. It came to his mind that he hadn't seen much of his own bogles lately, but he didn't miss them at all.

A week went by and then a second one and a third one. And the doctor found that instead of writing his learned book he'd be sitting and thinking how bright the red-haired lass's hair looked with the sun on it or how blue her eyes were or how the freckles looked on her saucy little nose. He was that homesick for her, he'd even have put up with the bogles, just to be at home, with her pouring out his tea and smiling at him from across the table.

So when she sent word at the end of the fourth week that he was to come back he went off so fast that he almost forgot to thank her grannie for having him and to say good-bye!

When he got back to his house he had to step out into the road and look well at it, for he wasn't sure it was his.

The windows were open from ground floor to garret, and all the heavy wooden blinds had been taken away entirely.

127

There were fresh white curtains blowing gently at all the windows and flowerpots on the sills.

Then the door opened and the red-haired lass stood in the doorway and smiled at him. It was his house after all!

"You've come then!" said she.

"I've come!" said he. And up the steps he went, two at a time. He could hardly believe 'twas the same place, when he saw what she'd done with it. Everything was light and bright, and through the whole house the fresh sea air blew, in one window and out another, so that the place was as sweet and fresh and wholesome as the red-haired lass herself.

"How about the bogles?" asked the doctor.

"They're gone," said the lass.

"All of them? Where did they go?" asked the doctor.

"Back to the Howff, I suppose," said the lass. "This isn't the sort of place bogles would be liking to bide in."

"No!" said the doctor, looking around. "I can see that for myself."

But he had one more question to ask, so he asked it. "Will you marry me?" he said.

"Of course I will!" said the red-haired lass. And she smiled at him and said, "Why else did you think I came here in the first place?"

So they were married, and the doctor had no more bogles in his house. But what he did have was half a dozen bairns, lads and lassies, all with red hair and blue eyes and saucy noses with freckles across them and merry smiles, just like their mother.

And bairns are better to fill a house with than bogles ever could be, so they all lived merrily ever after.